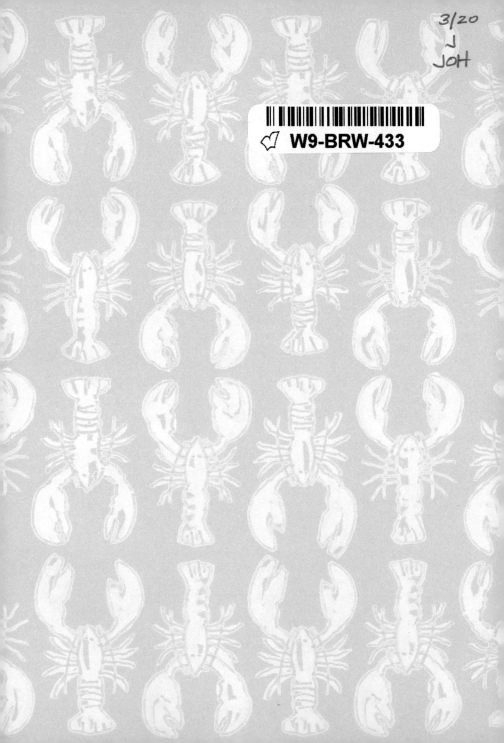

Beatrice Zinker

UPSIDE DOWN THINKER

SABOTAGE

by Shelley Johannes

DISNEY • HYPERION

LOS ANGELES   NEW YORK

For Bob—*my favorite partner in crime*

First Edition, March 2020
10 9 8 7 6 5 4 3 2 1
FAC-020093-20024
Printed in the United States of America

Text is set in Amsterdamer Garamont Pro/Fontspring
Designed by Phil Buchanan and Shelley Johannes
Illustrations created on tracing paper with felt-tip pen, brush marker, colored
pencil, a bit of licorice-scented Mr. Sketch, and a hint of Photoshop.

Library of Congress Control Number for Hardcover 2019945146

ISBN 978-1-4847-6740-5 (hardcover)
ISBN 978-1-4847-6816-7 (paperback)

Reinforced binding
Visit www.DisneyBooks.com

I

YO!

Beatrice Zinker checked up and down
the street five times, just to be sure,
then flashed a thumbs-up
at Lenny Santos.

The coast was
officially clear.

Not a car.

Not a bike.

Not even Mrs. Jenkins
walking her cat, Scrappy.

"Ready?" whispered Beatrice.

Lenny shifted into position.

"Ready," she said.

Moving as one, they dropped from the tree, snuck across Sam Darzi's roof, and crouched beside her bedroom window.

Beatrice raised her fist and gave the glass four quick taps, followed by two more. Just like they'd planned.

"Are you sure she's going to know it's us?"

"Positive," said Beatrice.

Who else would be on Sam's roof in a ninja suit, tapping HI in Morse code?

"Couldn't we just ring her doorbell?"

"We're a top-secret organization," said Beatrice. "And I've never met Sam's family. Ringing the doorbell would be weird."

"Isn't it weirder that you haven't met them? And we're on their roof again?"

A loud rap—single and precise—banged from the other side of the window.

Lenny's eyebrows rose.

Beatrice sat back on her heels and waited for the rest of the letter.

The windowpane rattled with a light tap, then shook again with two hard raps. A few seconds later, three more raps sounded against the glass.

"Yo!" Sam translated as she lifted the window. "I was starting to think you two weren't going to show."

She hoisted an old-fashioned typewriter over the windowsill.

Her black boots thudded onto the roof as Beatrice shrugged off her backpack and Lenny waved hello.

"We don't have much time," said Beatrice. "My dad will be back with the pizza soon."

It was Saturday night, and Pete Zinker was across town at Fetta's Pizzeria, getting their favorite special-occasion dinner. It wouldn't be long before his light blue Subaru came into view.

Beatrice offered Lenny the binoculars. "Want to be the lookout?"

Lenny's face lit up. "I love being the eyes of the operation." The strap looped over her neck. "When I see his car, I'll yell *Pepperoni*, loud and clear."

"Erfect-pay." Beatrice unzipped her bag. "Ready for attendance?"

A smirk played across Sam's face. "I'm pretty sure we're all here."

"She has a point," laughed Lenny.

Beatrice's gaze bounced around the circle. When she and Lenny cofounded Operation Upside at the end of last year, they were a two-agent operation, dedicated to celebrating the upside in everyone. Now that Sam had joined the team, they were a force of three.

"I officially call this meeting to order," Beatrice declared. "Since we're all here—as you can see."

Sam hauled the typewriter onto her lap. "Who has the supplies?"

Grinning, Beatrice dumped out the contents of her backpack. "I drew a bunch of new ones last night!" She passed an award to Sam.

Sam fed the piece of paper into the typewriter. The crisp certificate rolled around the cylinder. "Who's first?" Her fingers wriggled over the keys, waiting.

Lenny's hand shot into the air.

OooH ME!!

Beatrice knew exactly who Lenny was going to pick.

"I'm giving my award to Chloe," she announced. "Finally."

Lenny had been planning to give an UPSIDE to her new next-door neighbor, Chloe Llewelyn, since the beginning of the school year.

But every week, a different emergency came up
and the award went to someone else.

One week, it was Wes Carver.

One week, it was
a boy at the bus stop.

Last week, Grace Benjamin got braces.

"This is Chloe's week," said Lenny. "No matter what."

"What should it say?"

Lenny didn't hesitate. "Most Brave."

Beatrice blinked in surprise. When she pictured Chloe Llewelyn, several award-winning titles came to mind.

Most Bossy.

Most Squeamish.

Very Tall . . .

Most Brave wasn't one of them.

Lenny studied the doubt on Beatrice's face. "What?" she asked. "Starting a new school takes a lot of bravery. It's hard to make new friends."

Behind the typewriter, Sam's head bobbed in quiet agreement.

Her index finger punched the *M* key.

Letter by letter, Chloe's new title appeared.

As Sam typed, Lenny slowly spelled out Chloe's last name. Then Sam slid the award into a confidential envelope and passed it over to Lenny.

Just like that, it was official.

This week, Operation Upside would award Chloe Llewelyn for her bravery.

Beatrice passed Sam a new certificate. "This one's for you."

Sam chewed a strand of hair as she reloaded the typewriter.

Her boots bounced against the roof. "It can be anyone, right?"

Lenny's binoculars strayed from the street.

"Of course," Beatrice assured her.

Sam leaned over the keys. Her long hair shielded the award from view. Beatrice shrugged at Lenny as Sam's fingers tapped.

The rhythm of the keys was like a code of its own.

Curiosity grew with each peck and poke.

Finally, Sam pressed the lever and popped the award from the typewriter and sat back with a smile.

Beatrice and Lenny smiled back expectantly.

Instead of showing them, Sam slid the paper into a folder and pressed it closed.

Beatrice leaned forward. "Who's it for?"

Sam tucked the award under her leg. "This one's kind of private. . . . I'd rather not say."

The binoculars fell from Lenny's eyes. "Is that allowed?"

Beatrice shrugged. "I think so?"

Everything about Sam was kind of private. And Beatrice wasn't much of a rule-maker.

Especially this week.

When she had a secret of her own.

"To be honest . . ." Beatrice glanced at Sam. "I'm feeling kind of private this week too."

At the edge of the roof, Lenny groaned.

Sam nodded at Beatrice. "Thanks." She straightened the typewriter on her lap. "What should I type on yours?"

"You don't have to type mine." Beatrice grabbed a fresh certificate and slipped it into her bag. "I'm waiting for inspiration to strike. A blank one's fine."

Lenny removed her binoculars again.

"A blank one?" Her eyes narrowed. "Remember what happened last time?!"

Of course Beatrice remembered.

You don't forget something like that.

2
WHAT HAPPENED LAST TIME

"I remember it perfectly," Beatrice told Lenny.

She remembered holding ten blank awards, full of possibilities—and how excited she was to give the first one to her teacher, Mrs. Tamarack.

She remembered how Lenny wasn't sure it was a good idea . . . and how Mrs. Tamarack wasn't sure about it either.

But Beatrice remembered other parts, too.

Like when Sam
and her typewriter
saved the day.

Dear Mrs. Tamarack,

MOST STRICT was
meant to be a
compliment.

Sincerely,
X Anonymous

And how Operation Upside started as a duo,
but became a trio, and made a lot of people happy
that week.

"That was almost the end of us," Lenny sighed.

"But it turned out to be the beginning!" Beatrice cried.

Sam smiled under her hair.

"This is a recipe for disaster," Lenny huffed. "Not everything turns around!"

The Zinkers' light blue Subaru zoomed around a curve in the street below with its sunroof open and

its windows down. The evening breeze carried the crescendo of Pete Zinker's favorite symphony up to the rooftop and caught everyone's attention.

The three members of Operation Upside dropped their disagreement.

They reacted as one synchronized unit.

For Beatrice, it was a shout of relief.

Her dad arrived just in time.

If anything had the power to distract Lenny from possible recipes for disaster, it was Fetta's Pizza.

FETTA'S

BEST RECIPE FOR PIZZA IN THE MIDWEST

FOUR YEARS RUNNING

3
CIVILIANS

The truth was, Beatrice knew exactly who was getting her UPSIDE this week. She just couldn't talk about it in front of Sam.

And now telling Lenny would have to wait until dinner was over.

After leaving Sam's, Beatrice and Lenny scrambled across the street, crawled through Beatrice's bedroom window, and rushed downstairs to the kitchen, just as Pete Zinker burst through the door.

He raised an armload of pizza. "Who's ready for the Best Recipe for Pizza in the Midwest, Four Years Running?"

"Speaking of running . . ." Beatrice's mother, Nancy Zinker, stepped from behind the refrigerator door with a bowl of salad. "What were you guys doing up there? You look like you ran a marathon."

Lenny rested her hands on her knees and tried to catch her breath.

Pete Zinker grinned.

"Beatrice isn't sucking you into the world of breakdancing, is she, Lenny?"

"Guys!" Beatrice sighed. "You're ruining my surprise!"

Breakdancing was for after dinner.

When Lenny was in a better mood.

Nancy Zinker passed Beatrice a stack of plates. "Don't make Lenny watch that documentary, Beatrice. She doesn't want to sit through that."

Clearly her mother hadn't watched *Breaking the Mold: A Complete History of Hip-Hop*.

If she had, she would know you don't *sit through* a breakdancing documentary.

"Henry likes it." Beatrice pointed at her brother. "See?"

Her mother smiled wryly. "Is there a documentary Henry *doesn't* like?"

Pete Zinker flipped Beatrice's baby brother around and deposited him into his high chair. "That's my boy!"

He turned to Lenny. "Kate's at a sleepover tonight, so you get her spot." His hand gestured at the empty chair near Henry. "Right next to the King of Hip-Hop."

Beatrice plopped a plate on her brother's tray.

The official King of Hip-Hop was a highly debated topic, but she was positive Henry was not in the running.

Her brother's royal status wasn't worth worrying about tonight, though. There were three slices of Fetta's Pizza on her plate. Lenny was spending the night, Kate was at a sleepover, and right after dinner, she could finally tell Lenny her newest plan.

Midway through their meal, Nancy Zinker set down her fork. Her forehead creased with concern. "Are you feeling okay, Lenny?"

Beatrice paused mid-chew.

Her mother steepled her fingers under her chin. "I thought Fetta's was your favorite."

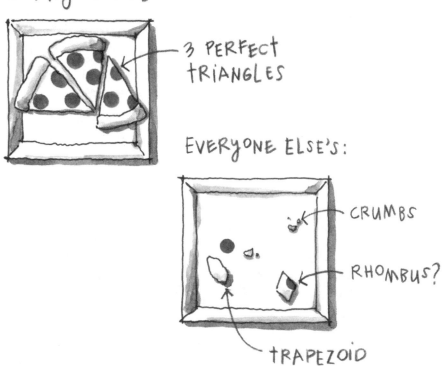

LENNY'S PLATE:

3 PERFECT TRIANGLES

EVERYONE ELSE'S:

CRUMBS

RHOMBUS?

TRAPEZOID

"It is!" Lenny stared at her plate. "I'm just not very hungry."

Guilt hit Beatrice in the chest.

Lenny usually lost her appetite when she was worried. Beatrice couldn't let her secret plan ruin Lenny's favorite dinner.

The Zinkers enforced a strict Don't Talk with Your Mouth Full rule. It was the only thing that saved Beatrice from blurting out the truth to Lenny right that second, in the presence of civilians.

KING OF THE CIVILIANS

CIVILIAN #1

CIVILIAN #2

CIVILIAN #3

Nancy Zinker felt Lenny's forehead. "Are you sure you're not sick?"

Beatrice rushed to swallow her bite. "She's fine, Mom! Everything's fine!"

Beatrice sent Lenny signals across the table.

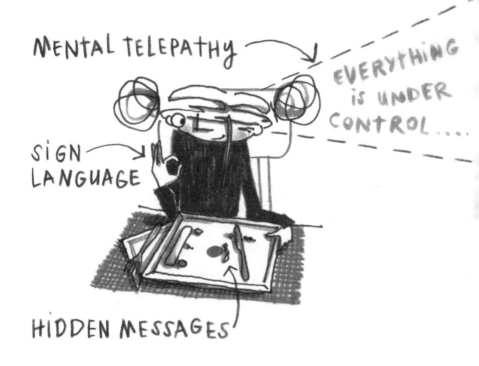

MENTAL TELEPATHY

EVERYTHING is UNDER CONTROL....

SIGN LANGUAGE

HIDDEN MESSAGES

Lenny didn't notice any of them.
She was too busy staring at her plate.

After Attempt #3, Beatrice deployed Plan B.

PLAN B

Tonight, Beatrice was grateful her mother believed in utensils. Even when the menu was pizza, each place setting received a full set of forks, spoons, and knives.

On the count of three, Beatrice's unused fork fell from her fingers with a crash. It clattered to the floor and clanged to a stop under Lenny's seat.

Beatrice bent under the table, pointing. "Lenny? Can you grab that for me?"

As soon as Lenny ducked down, Beatrice dropped her voice. "You should eat," she whispered. "I know exactly who's getting my award this week."

you
do?

"The faster you eat, the faster I can tell you."

Color returned to Lenny's face as they popped back up.

"Got my fork!" Beatrice exclaimed.

Nancy Zinker exchanged Beatrice's fork for a clean one. "I bet you'd feel better if you ate something, Lenny. I always say, 'Protein is the building block of life.'"

Lenny lifted one of her triangles for a giant bite. "I am a little hungry now."

Pete Zinker clinked his pizza against Lenny's. "Cheers," he said. "To Fetta's pizza, the building block of my life, many years running."

cLiNK

After that, Lenny inhaled her dinner.

As soon as she shoved a final bite into her mouth, Beatrice cleared their plates, and they skipped toward the stairs with Lenny still chewing.

Her dad laughed. "Where are you two going so fast?"

"Upstairs," said Lenny.

"Breakdancing," Beatrice chimed.

"I'll bring dessert up in a few minutes," her mother called. "In the meantime, don't break anything!"

Beatrice and Lenny, longtime partners in crime, hip-hopped up the stairs two at a time.

4

THE TRUTH

"Can you plug this in?" Beatrice passed Lenny a heavy-duty cord. "There's an outlet behind the dresser."

Lenny fished the cord down the wall until she found the plug. "What are we doing?"

Beatrice disappeared under her bunk. "I'll be right back," she called out.

Her shoes kicked wildly as she searched the space below Kate's mattress.

Moments later,
a scrap of cardboard
shot from under the bed
and spun toward Lenny's feet.
A flattened delivery box flew
out next. In seconds, an assortment of
cardboard covered the floor.

"What are we doing? Building a secret base?"
Lenny asked. "I thought you had something to say."

Beatrice wriggled from under the bed with a
pair of sneakers in her hands and a giant smile on
her face. "We're setting up the dance floor."

Lenny looked at the pile splayed around them.
As Lenny's hands settled on her hips, Beatrice
slipped on the sneakers and jumped to her feet.

"I do have something to tell you," Beatrice
insisted. "Right away!" She bent over a boxy stereo
and pressed PLAY.

Music boomed through the speakers. A heavy,
happy beat reverberated off the walls and pulsed
beneath their feet.

"My mom expects us to be breakdancing," Beatrice explained. "If it's too quiet up here, she'll get suspicious."

She turned a dial and the volume climbed.

The rhythm moved into her arms and her legs and took on a life of its own. For a minute, Beatrice forgot about secret plans and nervous friends and suspicious mothers.

There was only music . . .

. . . and moves.

"Whoa." From the look on Lenny's face, she'd forgotten her worries too. "Can you teach me that?"

Beatrice clapped. "I'd love to!"

STEP 1: STRETCH

STEP 2: GET iNTO POSiTiON

STEP 3: SPiN!

STEP 4: SPiN FASTER!

STEP 1: OUCH!

STEP 2: UGH.

STEP 3: WHOA...

STEP 4: OOF!

STEP 5:
FINISH WITH
FLAIR !

By the end of Lenny's lesson, their laughter was louder than the music.

Lenny pointed at Beatrice. "That was not as easy as you make it look."

The cardboard dance floor shifted as Beatrice dusted herself off. The heavy beat of the song matched the thud of her heart.

"I'm giving Sam my UPSIDE this week...."

Lenny lay flat on her back. "You are?"

"Yep," said Beatrice. "I know I'm giving it to Sam, but I'm not sure what it should say."

She'd been wracking her brain for days.

Lenny pushed her glasses back into place. "Most Mysterious?"

Beatrice wrinkled her nose. "Something nicer than that."

Lenny flipped over. "Don't you ever wonder why she's so secretive, though?"

"What do you mean?"

"I don't know," Lenny groaned. "Like, what if she's a spy for the other side?"

"What other side?"

Weren't they all on the same side?

Lenny didn't have an answer. "There's so much we don't know about her."

Beatrice shrugged. "Until last week, I never knew my dad used to listen to music on these."

RELIC #1: BOOMBOX

RELIC #2: CASSETTE TAPE

DANCE MIX

"That doesn't count. He's your dad."

"There's a lot of stuff you don't know about me," said Beatrice.

Lenny looked doubtful. "Like what?"

"Like—" Beatrice struck a new pose. "Did you know I do my best thinking upside down?"

Lenny scoffed. "Everyone knows that."

"Did you know I hum the ABCs backward while I brush my teeth?" she asked. "Or that I even breakdance in my sleep?"

Lenny propped on her elbows. "Did I tell you my lola's teaching me to knit?" she asked. "So far, I've made eight hats."

"I've been trying to master mental telepathy," said Beatrice. "So far, no luck."

Lenny touched her temples. "What am I thinking right now?"

"Um . . ." Beatrice's eyes closed in concentration. "That you wish my mom would show up with brownies?"

"Knock, knock!" a voice yelled from the top of the stairs. "Is everyone in one piece up there?"

As Nancy Zinker peeked through the doorway, the fudgy smell of warm brownies filled the room.

She set a plate between them, turned down the music, and retreated with a smile. "Don't forget to brush your teeth when you're done with these."

Later that night, after they had transformed the dance floor into a fort and gotten cozy in their sleeping bags, Lenny flicked on her flashlight in the darkness. Its beam illuminated Beatrice's face.

"Are you still awake?"

Beatrice opened her eyes.

"Remember how it used to be?" Lenny whispered. "When Operation Upside was just you and me?"

Beatrice nodded.

Lenny had been the other half of Operation Upside from the very beginning. And they'd been an unstoppable duo since first grade, way before they had an official organization.

Lenny's pillow rustled in the darkness. Her flashlight trembled on the ceiling. "Things are so different now."

Shadows danced above their heads as Beatrice pondered Lenny's words.

Things *were* different.

Before this school year, she and Lenny were inseparable. Just the two of them, like there was no one else in the world.

Now there was Chloe.

And there was Sam.

Recess meant playing veterinarian instead of top-secret adventure, and Operation Upside was a trio instead of a duo.

Beatrice smiled at her first partner in crime. "We're still really good at this though." Her fingers formed a heart and borrowed the beam on Lenny's flashlight.

"Cofounders forever."

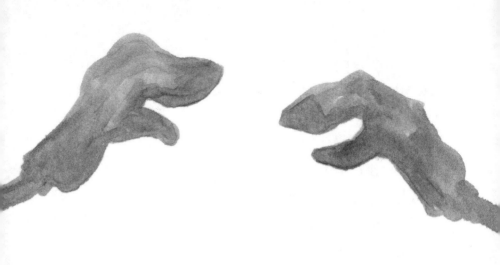

Eventually Lenny dimmed her flashlight and their shadow puppets faded into the night. She folded her arms behind her head. "Chloe's going to be really happy when she gets her UPSIDE this week."

Beatrice snuggled into her blankets as a yawn took over her face. "When are you delivering it?"

"Monday at recess," said Lenny. "I might need your help with a tiny distraction."

Beatrice sat up.

All her sleepiness fell away.

"I'm good at distractions!"

"Nothing major," Lenny clarified. "Just a tiny one."

Possibilities twinkled in Beatrice's wide-awake eyes. Her smile glowed in the dark. "This week is going to be legendary."

"Tiny," Lenny repeated.

Beatrice nestled into her pillow.

Her brain began dreaming up distractions before her lashes fully closed.

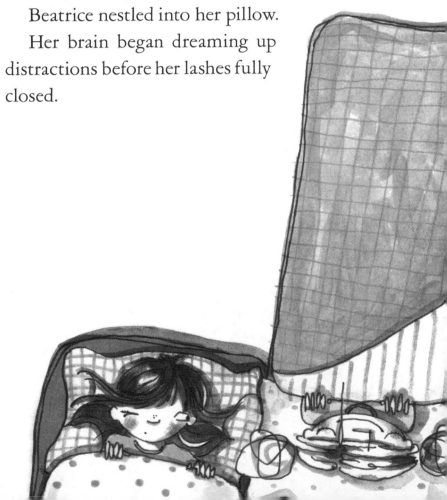

5

SMALL-ISH

Monday morning, Beatrice woke up full of ideas.

Unfortunately, none of them were tiny.

She brainstormed through breakfast,
and on the bus, and in class, but when
the bell rang for recess, her ideas
were at an impasse.

Beatrice followed the
recess crowd as they
trampled to the back of
the playground. Maybe
the perfect tiny idea would
pop up in her travels.

After a trek through the trees, the landscape
cleared and a wooden play structure appeared.
Beatrice dropped into her best thinking position
and surveyed the scene.

Chloe Llewelyn—the school's Most Brave newcomer—was stationed in the doorway, under a sign labeled VET. A long line of pretend pet owners, and their adorable make-believe pets, was quickly forming in front of her.

In Chloe's first week at William Charles Elementary, her veterinary clinic became the most popular game on the playground.

Lenny darted over to Beatrice. "Ready whenever you are," she whispered.

Beatrice pointed at the bag slung over Lenny's shoulder. "Is it in there?"

"Safe and sound," said Lenny. "I'm going to sneak it into her clipboard when I get your cue."

With a wave, she spun on her heel and walked away. "See you in a few."

Beatrice watched Lenny wander inside, until her friend Wes Carver arrived at her side.

"Don't tell me," he said, unloading an armful of art supplies. "I think I can get this one."

Ever since Chloe made Wes her official veterinary assistant, every recess started with a guessing game. He didn't win often, but he loved to play Guess Beatrice's Upside-Down-Animal-of-the-Day.

Wes circled her with a squinted eye. "Are you an opossum?"

Wes was the only third-grader who knew more upside down animals than Beatrice. He'd watched more documentaries than Henry and Beatrice combined.

He wasn't going to win today's game, though.

Because Beatrice wasn't anything yet. She was just herself, upside down, trying to think of a tiny distraction.

"Maybe a magpie?"

Beatrice shook her head.

"A salamander?"

"Nope," said Beatrice. "Good try."

His head tilted to the side. "Gecko? Wombat?"

Beatrice laughed. "Wombats don't even go upside down."

"If you were a wombat, they would."

Wes tapped his chin.

Then his temple.

Then his toe.

He was running out of guesses, and Beatrice was running out of time.

"Wait!" Wes exclaimed. "Are you a *Cassiopea* jellyfish?!"

Beatrice brightened. "A what?"

"A *Cassiopea* jellyfish. It's this giant jellyfish that swims upside down."

"Are you sure that's a thing?"

It sounded like the coolest creature ever.

"PBS did a show about them last week. They're so amazing, it's hard to believe they're brainless."

"Brainless?" Beatrice repeated. "What's the point of being upside down if you can't even *think*?"

"Maybe they think in a different way?"

A different-thinking, upside down jellyfish?

Beatrice's whole body zipped with excitement. Then she asked the most important detail. . . .

"Are they tiny?"

Wes shrugged. "Small-ish?"

Beatrice flopped to the ground and flailed around. "We have a winner!"

Wes snapped his fingers. "I knew it!"

With her limbs wiggling and jiggling, Beatrice gave a little moan. "I'm a different-thinking, upside down jellyfish and I desperately need a veterinarian. Can you get me inside?"

Lenny needed one tiny moment to deliver Chloe's award. One tiny moment when everyone was looking at Beatrice, and no one was paying attention to Lenny.

Especially Chloe.

Wes stuffed his hands into his sweatshirt. "If I say the word JELLYFISH in front of Chloe, she'll fire me on the spot."

Beatrice glanced at the notice posted beside the clinic door.

ORDINARY PETS ONLY!

NO MONKEYS ALLOWED!

NO Kinkajous please

NO KANGAROOS

"You're right," Beatrice agreed. "She might."

Luckily, her plan would work just as well without Wes.

"I'll go in unannounced," she said. As all good distractions do.

6
TINY DANCER

Luckily Beatrice knew *exactly* how an upside down jellyfish would make an entrance if it lived on land and had arms and legs instead of tentacles.

CRABWALK

THE FLOAT

CRAZY LEGS

JELLYFISH FLARE

TENTACLE
TANGLE

When Chloe screamed, "I got an award!"
Beatrice knew her tiny performance was complete.

Chloe was standing up front, clipboard in hand,
looking taller than ever.

Lenny stood beside her, smiling.

Behind Chloe's head—among an ever-growing collection of veterinary rules—was a brand-new piece of paper.

The *Cassiopea* jellyfish did a tiny victory dance. Her distraction had worked!

A curious crowd of pets encircled Chloe.

They went from crawling on all fours to standing on tiptoe, peeking at the award. Their barking and meowing became oohing and aahing.

As Beatrice edged between them for a closer view, alarm bells blared in her head.

Something wasn't right.

Chloe's award was supposed to say MOST BRAVE, not BEST VET. Sam had typed the words MOST BRAVE, right in front of them.

Why were different words typed there now?

Beatrice's gaze flew to Lenny.

She was smiling the most fake smile Beatrice had ever seen.

When Lenny really smiled, her eyes crinkled up like they were smiling too.

ZERO CRINKLE

Something definitely wasn't right.

Chloe cleared her throat and addressed the crowd. "I've gotten a lot of awards in my life, but this is the most official." Her fingertips brushed the letters. "It's typed and everything."

Lenny stood there, looking pale.

Her eyes not at all crinkly.

Opinions and observations spouted from the crowd.

"Where'd it come from?" asked Parvati.

Eva shuffled forward to investigate. "Who made it?"

Lenny's fake smile slipped into a frown. When her eyes found Beatrice in the crowd, she mouthed two desperate words. "Kinkajou Fever."

Every secret organization needs an emergency phrase—something to signal that everything has gone wrong. For Operation Upside, that phrase was Kinkajou Fever.

Lips were hard to read, though.

Lenny might have been saying something else.

They needed a meeting, and they needed one now. Unfortunately, before Beatrice could reach her, Chloe pulled Lenny aside for a meeting of her own.

"Word about this award will travel fast," Chloe whispered. "The clinic's about to get even busier, and we need a plan." Her voice dropped lower. "If a business doesn't prepare for success, things quickly fall apart."

As Chloe's voice grew even quieter, Beatrice leaned closer.

Chloe jumped when she saw her. "Beatrice!" she screamed. "What are you doing?"

Beatrice waved up at her. "I'm a *Cassiopea* jellyfish."

Chloe shuddered and then looked around. "Where's Wes?" She called out the door, "Wes?"

Wes came around the corner. "Yes?"

She grabbed her clipboard and clicked her pen. "We need more rules."

Wes peered down at Beatrice.

Curiosity smirked across his face.

"Here." Chloe ripped off a sheet of paper and tossed it to Wes. "Let's start with these."

Two things got Wes the job as Chloe's assistant. His vast knowledge of animals was one thing. His impressive collection of scented art supplies was the other.

Spinning on her toes, Chloe turned back to the crowd. "We'll get to each of you as soon as we can. Please be patient as we navigate these exciting new waters."

She frowned at Beatrice and scribbled another note.

Wes and Beatrice waded out of the clinic's exciting waters into the calm outside.

Wes raised his eyebrows.

"What's going on in there?"

He unrolled a new poster from his supplies and splayed his markers on the ground.

"I'm not exactly sure." Beatrice grabbed another poster and joined him in the grass. "Chloe got an award. That's all I know."

Wes looked up. An open marker was clamped between his teeth. "She did?"

"Yep," said Beatrice. "BEST VET."

Wes lifted up a bright blue marker. "Does this look like a good jellyfish color?"

Beatrice brought the marker close. "Perfect."

It was a good blue, and it smelled good too.

Wes took his marker back. "Is Chloe's award like Mrs. Tamarack's?"

"That's what everyone was saying."

Everyone except Lenny—who may have been saying Kinkajou Fever.

"I need to ask Lenny more at lunch."

While Wes colored, Beatrice strained her ears, listening for Mrs. Tamarack's end-of-recess whistle.

Lunch couldn't come soon enough.

7

MEAT LOAF TO THE RESCUE

Beatrice's brain tumbled with questions as she entered the cafeteria.

Where did the BEST VET award come from?

Did Lenny really say Kinkajou Fever?

Was Operation Upside in a state of emergency?

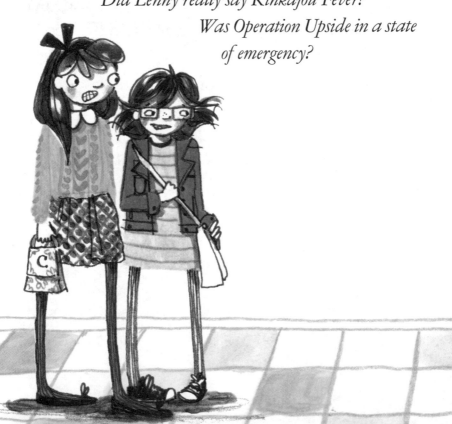

The biggest question on her mind was how to get Lenny alone so they could talk. Ten steps behind her, Chloe was stuck to Lenny like glue, and it didn't look like she was letting go anytime soon.

Then, like a giant arrow pointing the way, the cafeteria bulletin board came into view.

MEAT LOAF &
MASHED POTATOES

THIS WAY

"Lenny, look!" Beatrice exclaimed.

Lenny and Chloe paused in mid-step.

Eva and Parvati skidded to a stop behind them.

"Meat loaf and mashed potatoes?" Chloe dropped Lenny's arm and retreated a step. A shudder coursed through her. "Who comes up with these menus?"

Beatrice stood near the arrow. "Meat loaf's not for everyone, but Lenny likes it almost as much as I do. Right, Lenny?"

Silently, Beatrice chanted *Meat loaf* over and over, begging Lenny to say yes. If only she had conquered telepathic communication. Sending messages with her mind would be so handy.

Wait. Maybe there *was* a way.

Beatrice looked straight at Lenny, locked eyes, and blinked her eyelashes.

Letter by letter, flitter by flutter, she spelled out MEAT LOAF in Morse code.

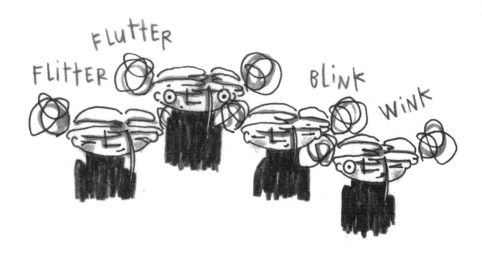

An odd look—part confusion, part curiosity—
crossed Lenny's face.

Chloe retreated another step. "Is something
wrong with your eyes?"

Beatrice shook her head. "I don't think so."

"Maybe it's allergies," said Chloe. "My mom
said the pollen count is really high today."

Beatrice leaned against the wall, where a
surprising number of students stood in line. "I'm
hoping meat loaf will help. My mom says protein
is the building block of life."

Beatrice blinked MEAT LOAF at Lenny, one more time, to be extra clear.

"My mom says '*Bahala na*,'" joked Lenny. "Today I think that means, 'Get the meat loaf.'"

"Okay . . ." said Chloe, backing away.

As Chloe left, Beatrice sagged. "Thank goodness you knew what I was blinking."

"Whenever you're acting weird, I just follow along." Lenny's eyes darkened. "Plus, we *really* need to talk."

"Kinkajou Fever?" Beatrice whispered.

Lenny nodded grimly. "WE'VE BEEN SABOTAGED."

Cafeteria noises buzzed as Beatrice reached for a tray. "Didn't your award say MOST BRAVE?"

"It still does," said Lenny.

She swung her bag around. Chloe's award peeked out of the pocket. MOST BRAVE was typed across the top, just like Beatrice remembered.

"I have no idea who made that other one." Lenny bit her lip, and then blinked at Beatrice. "Was it you?"

Beatrice stared at her friend. "Me?" She lifted her tray to receive a loaf of meat.

"It's okay if it was. . . ."

The lunch lady raised a ladle. "Gravy, dear?"

Beatrice nodded without thinking.

Lenny lifted her shoulder. "Maybe you got too excited, or thought I was taking too long?"

"You think I did it?"

Brown liquid flooded Beatrice's plate.

"Sorry." Lenny stared at her tray. "I had to ask."

Beatrice shook her head.

It didn't feel very good, but she understood.

Lenny's gaze meandered across the room and landed on the third member of their secret operation. Sam Darzi was sitting at her normal table, hidden behind a giant book, camouflaged among fourth-grade boys.

"You don't think that Sam . . . ?"

Lenny's question dangled, unfinished.

"Sam?" said Beatrice. "No way." Her meat loaf jiggled on her tray. "Why would she?"

Lenny shrugged. "Why wouldn't she?"

A few weeks ago, Beatrice didn't trust Sam either. Mystery was practically her middle name. In fact, Beatrice had no idea what Sam's middle name was. But now she knew you don't have to know everything about someone before you trust them.

"What if this was her plan all along?" Lenny wondered out loud.

Sam looked up from her book and shot a smile in their direction.

"It wasn't Sam," Beatrice insisted. "Give me one day. I'll collect clues and prove it to you." Her tray shifted to her hip. "Please don't ask Sam about this. We're just getting to know her. If she thinks we don't trust her, it would ruin everything. I just need one day to figure this out."

"One day?" Lenny looked skeptical.

Beatrice grimaced. "How about two?"

"Fine—two," Lenny agreed. "I don't know if you're going to like what you find out, though. Because if it wasn't you, and it wasn't Sam, then who?"

Beatrice scanned the faces in the cafeteria. "That's a really good question."

8
ANOTHER GOOD QUESTION

Lenny frowned at her tray of meat loaf and asked another good question. "Do we actually have to eat this?"

Beatrice grimaced at her gravy. "I think we do." Her neck craned toward their lunch table. "Since Chloe's our best eyewitness, let's go get some clues."

Chloe scooted her chair to make room as they approached. "I could smell you guys a mile away." Her nose scrunched. "Meat loaf. Even the name's gross." She popped the lid on a square container and grabbed an orange wedge. "Didn't you bring your lunch, Lenny?"

"I did, but . . ." Color flooded Lenny's cheeks. "Meat loaf suddenly sounded good."

Chloe glanced at Lenny's plate, not looking convinced. She slid her container of oranges between them. "I'll leave these here, in case you change your mind. Just save a few for Grace. They're her favorite. . . ."

Chloe's voice trailed off as she scanned the table. "Where is she, anyway?"

Lenny swallowed a mouthful of mashed potatoes. "Orthodontist appointment."

"Aw, again? I really wanted to tell her about my award." Chloe nibbled a string of cheese. "Is she coming back?"

Beatrice leaned forward.

She needed to take control of the conversation. Chloe was supposed to be answering questions. Not asking them.

"So—Chloe," Beatrice said. "Did you see who gave you the award?"

Chloe's face lit up. "No! I barely noticed it at first. It looked so natural on the wall with everything else. You know?"

Beatrice and Lenny nodded and took heaping bites of meat loaf to prevent themselves from talking. *Not* talking was the best way to get a witness to *keep* talking.

If you stayed quiet, you could learn a lot.

Chloe grabbed another orange and leaned back in her seat. "My award looks exactly like Mrs. Tamarack's. What do you think that means?" A hopeful glaze lit her eyes. "Do you think she made it for me?"

Beatrice raised her eyebrows. Mrs. Tamarack didn't seem like the award-giving type.

The rest of the table shrugged in unison.

Parvati sipped her juice box. "It was really nice of whoever it was."

"I know," Chloe agreed. "My mom's going to freak out. Did you know she's an award-winning veterinarian, too?"

A FELINE SPECIALIST, ACTUALLY.

An extra chair squeezed up to the table.

"Hi!" Grace greeted everyone.

"Ooh," said Eva. She pointed at Grace's braces. "You got purple this time!"

Grace grinned while the girls admired her new rubber bands. "What'd I miss?"

The whole table talked at once. Chloe wasn't the only one eager to retell the BEST VET story to fresh ears.

Unfortunately, no one added fresh details.

Grace helped herself to Chloe's oranges. "You definitely deserve that award. What did we even do at recess before you came?"

When lunch ended, Chloe led the way back to class, still reliving the thrill of the moment. Lenny and Beatrice lagged behind at the trash.

"That was a bust." Lenny dumped her half-eaten meat loaf into the garbage. "The only lead was Mrs. Tamarack, and I doubt she had anything to do with it." Lenny stood aside so Beatrice could reach the bin. "Sam still makes the most sense to me."

"Sam did not sabotage us."

"How would anyone else know I planned to give Chloe that award?"

"I'm not sure yet." Beatrice wiped her hands, feeling determined. "Can you get me into the vet clinic next recess? I need a better look at that award."

The scene of a crime is the best place to gather clues.

There could be fingerprints.
Footprints.
All kinds of things.

Lenny sighed. "Operation Upside was so much easier when it was just you and me."

She rummaged through her bag and produced a headband. "Take this," she told Beatrice. "If you're willing to be a cat, I can get you inside."

9

AN INSIDE JOB

Before they entered Classroom 3B, Lenny tugged Beatrice's sleeve. "Before I can get you inside," she whispered, "you have to make it outside."

She tapped the poster beside them.

Beatrice glinted out the window. "My eyes are on the prize."

Her eyes would also be on the clock. Second recess started at two o'clock, on the dot.

Beatrice remained right-side-up for the first thirty-seven minutes of the afternoon.

The class was so quiet during Read to Self that Mrs. Tamarack gave them each a sticker and grabbed a game from the Brain Break shelf.

Beatrice flew through the first round.

She survived the second.

But the third round was too much fun.

In Social Studies, her downhill luck continued.

Lenny met her eyes from across the room. "Stay on two," she mouthed.

The words became a chant in Beatrice's head. *Stay on two. Whatever you do, stay on two.*

She stayed on two
through all
of Writing.

She stayed on two through most of Science.

She would have made it all the way through, if Jeremy Galapagos hadn't stuck a cotton swab up his nose. How was anyone expected to make it through that?

BA
HA HA
HA
HA HA HA

"Two and a half?" Beatrice asked.

It seemed too good to be true.

Mrs. Tamarack crossed her arms. "Would you like the other half?"

"No," said Beatrice.

"Let's just get through Math. Do you think you can do that?"

Beatrice snuck a glance at Sam, sitting in the back. She faced her teacher. "Yes, I can do that."

"Good," said Mrs. Tamarack. Her shoes clicked to the board at the front of the room. "We're starting a new unit today."

Making it through Math right-side-up was one thing. Making it through *multiplication* was another.

Even the weather complained.

Outside the classroom window, the hopeful blue day turned an ominous gray.

Five minutes into the lesson, Beatrice's brain was as cloudy and confused as the sky outside.

Somehow if you turned a plus sign sideways, numbers got bigger faster. 8 and 8 equaled 64, instead of 16. And 3 and 4 equaled 12, not 7.

It made no sense.

Finally, after example upon example, Mrs. Tamarack capped her marker. "I think that's enough for one day."

Beatrice slumped in relief.

Technically, she was still on two.

And *a half*.

The class jumped up and jumbled into line. As Beatrice joined them, the gray sky thundered, deep and ominous. Everyone froze as lightning flashed and the windows rattled in their frames.

All at once, the clouds burst open and recess went down the drain.

Mrs. Tamarack sighed. "Apparently, class, we're staying inside."

10

UNO, DOS, DOS ½

The rain came down—loud and lots.

Beatrice rested her head on her desk and tried to regroup. Even if she couldn't get outside for recess, she could still hunt for clues.

The award-giving impostor was probably right in the room, stuck with indoor recess too.

As casually as possible, Beatrice sat up and scanned her classmates for anything out of the ordinary.

Just like certain kids played veterinarian during outdoor recess—while Sam scribbled in her notebook, and everyone else played soccer—people had predictable indoor routines too.

A few kids flocked to the puzzles.

Owen and André set up chess.

The veterinary crew gathered around Chloe. They made new and improved headbands while Chloe brainstormed a bigger business plan and dictated more rules to Wes.

The remainder of the class gathered on the carpet to watch Ms. Frizzle and her magic school bus zoom away.

Only one person was acting abnormal. . . .

Sam.

Instead of shuffling her boots toward the back of the room, she was walking toward Beatrice, shuffling a deck of cards.

Pre-Approved Pets:
✓ Dogs
✓ Cats
✓ Rabbits
✗ Anything else!

Nothing Gross!

She offered Beatrice a wobbly smile. "Want to play?"

STRANGELY— you CAN'T PLAY THIS ALONE....

"Yes!" said Beatrice, already clearing her desk.

Sam destroyed her, four hands in a row.

Beatrice didn't care, though.

Her mind was too busy concocting a plan to clear Sam's name. Rain or shine, she had to get outside before the evidence was lost for good.

By the time Sam declared her final victory, Beatrice knew exactly how she was going to get back to the vet clinic at the end of the day.

The weather had laid down a SKIP or two— but Beatrice had a WILD CARD up her sleeve.

II

WILD CARD

Beatrice didn't share her plan with anyone.

Every day after school, the buses sat in the parking lot for five long minutes before heading on their routes.

Beatrice's plan hinged on all five of those minutes.

> 2 minutes to get to vet clinic.
> 1 minute to catalog clues.
> + 2 minutes to get back to the bus.
> _____
> 5 quick minutes.

That was Beatrice's kind of math.

When the bell rang, a parade of umbrellas bobbed toward their buses. Nobody noticed when one umbrella stepped off the path and raced for the trees.

The rain was more drizzle than downpour now, but by the time Beatrice reached the back corner of the playground, her ninja suit was drenched with mud and rain.

She squinted at the schoolyard behind her, not sure how much time had passed.

The buses were little yellow dots on the horizon. The faint rumble of their idling engines reverberated across the grass. Hoping she was still on track, Beatrice turned toward the vet clinic.

Collecting clues wasn't going to be easy.

A puddle wrapped around the perimeter of the play structure like a moat. If there had been any evidence on the ground, it was long gone.

Hopping over the moat, Beatrice ducked through the doorway.

Inside the clinic it was dim and damp, but still a welcome shelter from the wet outside. Beatrice squeezed her dripping buns and wiped the water from her eyes.

As her vision adjusted to the room, Chloe's wall of rules came into view.

She stepped closer and blinked in despair.

Chloe's counterfeit award was supposed to be right there.

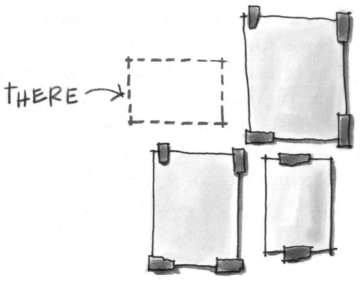

THERE →

Like the clues outside, it was gone.

Every rule and banned-pet poster remained, but where Chloe's award used to be, there was nothing. Not even a remnant of duct tape.

Beatrice glanced down at her feet.

She spun in a circle and kicked the mud. She flipped upside down and searched the ceiling.

But no award.

If it wasn't on the wall, it wasn't on the ceiling, and it wasn't on the ground, where in the world was it?

More importantly—who took it?

Beatrice stared at the gaping award-sized hole until a familiar rumble rattled across the playground.

The rumble wasn't the quiet vibration of waiting bus engines. It was louder than that.

It was the sound buses make while driving away.

12

MISSING!

WAit!!/\.

Beatrice hurdled the moat and ran outside, hoping she was wrong, hoping the thunder had returned.

But it wasn't thunder.

The yellow dots at the front of the building were moving.

The buses were leaving without her.

This time Beatrice skipped the trees.

She raced through the grass, waving her arms and yelling at the top of her lungs.

Her voice evaporated into the rain and the distance.

She ran harder.

Her arms pumped.

Her legs leaped.

Her lungs burned as she ran.

She ran until slippery grass became concrete playground.

Until concrete became sidewalk.

But she wasn't fast enough.

When her feet reached the curb, the last speck of yellow disappeared down the street. Beatrice was huffing and puffing and drenched straight through.

Her arms drooped at her sides.

Her backpack slid down her shoulders.

Her umbrella sagged to the ground.

Soon, panic set in.

She'd been lost before—but she'd never been left behind.

Defeated, she collapsed on the curb.

Her bottom landed in a puddle, and her face crumpled. Between gulps, Beatrice reminded herself to think.

Concentrate. Concentrate, she told herself.

Her mind was completely blank.

Not a thought.

Not a plan.

Not an inkling of anything.

Hot tears plopped into a puddle at her feet.

Her bus was gone.

Chloe's award was missing.

And if she didn't figure out who sabotaged Operation Upside by tomorrow, Lenny was going to say something to Sam. Once she did, there'd be no going back.

Instead of being close to solving the mystery, the answer seemed further and further away.

A dark minivan eased up to the curb.

Its tinted window rolled down.

"Beatrice?"

The side door slid open, and a long shadow passed over Beatrice's face. A pair of black boots stepped into the puddle next to her.

A familiar voice said, "I thought it was you."

13

AN EXTRACTION

Sam Darzi squatted next to Beatrice.

"Hey," she said. "Everything okay?" Her boots shifted in the puddle. "Need an extraction?"

Beatrice blinked. "A what?"

Sam's gaze traveled down the curb, where Mrs. Tamarack paced on bus duty, mostly hidden under a giant umbrella. Her purposeful, click-clacking stride was heading their way.

Sam nodded at the van. "Do you need an emergency exit?"

Beatrice's eyes widened. "Mrs. Tamarack's on bus duty?"

Next to them, the side door of the vehicle stood open. Sam's eyebrows rose. "Hop inside if you want a ride." She dove into the minivan without waiting for a reply.

Beatrice vaulted after her.

As they toppled inside, Sam slammed the door and Beatrice ducked out of sight. "Go, go, go!" said Sam, waving her mother forward.

Mrs. Darzi, however, did not go.

At least not very far—or very fast.

The minivan edged away from the curb and angled into the first open parking space.

Sam's mom glared into the rearview mirror. "We're not going anywhere until you tell me what's going on," she said. "I can't let any odd kid jump into my car and speed away."

Sam sighed. "She's not any odd kid. It's Beatrice, Mom."

Her mom released her seat belt and turned to face them. "Beatrice Zinker?"

The corner of Sam's mouth lifted. "Mom, this is Beatrice." She turned to Beatrice. "Beatrice, this is my mom."

A dimpled smile lit up Mrs. Darzi's face. "It's so nice to finally meet you!" Her warm voice felt like a hug. "Sam's told me so much about you."

Sam balanced her backpack between her boots. "Beatrice missed her bus. Can we drive her home?"

Beatrice looked down at her muddy shoes and her muddy jeans and her muddy everything.

Her eyes met Mrs. Darzi's.

"I'm kind of . . . muddy."

"No worry at all," Mrs. Darzi assured her. "I'm more concerned about other things. Like, is there someone we should call?"

Mrs. Darzi held up her phone.

Beatrice nodded.

"My mom, maybe?"

"Do you know her number?"

"If I type it, I do."

Beatrice flipped Mrs. Darzi's phone upside down and punched her mom's number.

The phone rang and rang and rang, and eventually went to voicemail. Mrs. Tamarack was still pacing the sidewalk in the rain, so Beatrice frantically dialed again.

On her third attempt, Nancy Zinker picked up. "Hello?"

"Hi, Mom."

"Beatrice?!" Her mom's voice rose three octaves. "What'd you do?! Are you hurt? Where are you?!"

It was hard to know where to start.

Her mom shouted, "Never mind. Stay put. I'm on my way!"

"Wait!" said Beatrice. "Sam's mom can drive me home. Is that okay?"

The line went quiet for a moment.

Then, "Who's Sam? Sam *who*?!" Her question broadcast loud enough for the whole car.

Sam picked at her boots while Mrs. Darzi pretended not to hear.

Wipers squeaked across the windshield.

"Sam Darzi," Beatrice clarified. "The girl who lives across the street."

Face on fire, she handed the phone to Mrs. Darzi. "She wants to talk to you."

While the grown-ups sorted things out, Beatrice snuck an occasional glance at Sam, who snuck an occasional glance at Beatrice. They both kept an occasional eye on Mrs. Tamarack, who, after pacing back and forth on the sidewalk, was finally heading inside.

Mrs. Darzi set down her phone and shifted into reverse. "You officially have a ride."

Beatrice clicked her seat belt and tried to relax.

Mrs. Darzi glanced in the mirror. "Sam told me about your club."

Beatrice straightened. Her eyes darted to Sam. She told her mom about Operation Upside?

Sam shook her head back and forth, while her mom continued talking.

"I wish someone had started a foreign-language club when I was in school," said Mrs. Darzi. "Did Sam tell you she speaks four languages?"

You do?

"Sam said you speak several too. How many do you speak?"

Beatrice looked to Sam, uncertain how to answer.

Sam leaned forward. "Three, if you count Pig Latin and Puppet. Four, if you count Morse code."

She looked amused.

Mrs. Darzi looked confused.

After that, the car slipped into quiet.

A familiar patchwork of houses and trees blurred past Beatrice's window. Sam's head disappeared into one of her books. Her mom flipped on the radio.

Two songs later, when they pulled up to Sam's house, Mrs. Darzi turned around. "How wonderful you live right across the street, Beatrice. I'm glad Sam has a friend."

"Mom . . ." Sam groaned.

Guilt punched Beatrice in the gut.

There was no way Lenny was right about Sam.

Sam pointed down the road.

"Here they come. . . ."

Nancy Zinker's gray van careened into Beatrice's driveway. Gravel scattered under its wheels. Her dad's car spun in close behind.

As their car doors flew open, Henry's babysitter, Daphne, rushed outside to meet them.

On the corner, three houses down, the school bus pulled away from the curb. Kate broke away from her friends and sprinted down the sidewalk.

Everyone's eyes were zeroed in on the same target.

Mrs. Darzi's door cracked open.

"Come on," she offered softly. "I'll walk you home."

Nodding, Beatrice gulped.

As the side door clicked open, Sam reached for the bright yellow backpack at her feet. "I have something for you."

The commotion outside faded away.

For a brief moment, Beatrice imagined Sam pulling Chloe's missing award out of her backpack, a smirk on her face, saying the whole thing was just a joke.

"You still have my flag book, right?"

Sam wasn't holding an UPSIDE. Instead she pressed a folded slip of paper into Beatrice's hand. "Don't look now," she told her.

To keep herself from peeking, Beatrice shoved the note deep into her pocket.

Her eyes drifted across the street.

A wry smile quirked on Sam's lips. "How much trouble are you in?"

"A lot, I think."

Sam's smile softened in sympathy.

Beatrice hoisted her backpack over her shoulder. With a shaky breath, she hopped from the van and accepted Mrs. Darzi's outstretched hand.

"Good luck," Sam called out.

"Thanks," said Beatrice.

Judging from the size of the crowd gathered in her driveway, she was going to need it.

14

GROUNDED

The Zinkers squeezed Beatrice like she'd been gone forever. They showered her with kisses and tears and too many I-love-yous.

Suddenly, crushed in their familiar arms, Beatrice was as relieved to see her family as they were to see her.

She closed her eyes and hugged and kissed and I-love-you-ed right back.

Eventually her parents stepped aside so Kate could hug her too.

Once they'd thanked Mrs. Darzi and their collective fears were eased, the family meandered inside. In the kitchen, Nancy Zinker smiled at Kate. "Would you please find Beatrice something dry to wear?"

Pete Zinker pulled out a chair and suggested Beatrice take a seat. "Before we talk to the principal again, we need to know what happened."

Beatrice's tongue stuck in her throat.

"The principal?"

Her parents took the chairs across from her.

"Yes, the principal," said her mother. "No one knew where you were."

Beatrice shook her head miserably. "It's my own fault. I thought I had enough time."

"Enough time for what?" her dad wanted to know.

Her fingertip traced the grain of the tabletop. "I was trying to solve a mystery. . . ."

Her parents' eyes met. This wasn't their first kitchen table conversation about missions and mysteries.

Nancy Zinker cleared her throat. "That ninja suit gets you into a lot of trouble, Beatrice."

"It was just a mistake!"

It wasn't the ninja suit's fault.

"Don't be surprised if Mrs. Klein calls you to her office tomorrow. This kind of mistake cannot happen again." Her mother's chair scooted from the table. "Let's get that outfit in the wash."

Kate came down the stairs with a pile of pajamas outstretched for Beatrice.

Nancy Zinker smiled. *"Merci beaucoup."*

Kate huffed. "Please tell me she's grounded."

Her dad patted her shoulder. "We've got this under control, Kate."

In the laundry room, Beatrice relinquished her favorite outfit. Her mother uncapped the detergent. "Why don't you go wash up while I work on all these muddy spots?"

"Okay," Beatrice agreed.

In the bathroom mirror, Beatrice took her time. She plucked stray leaves from her tangled hair, smoothed the wrinkles in her pajamas, and smudged the mud off her chin.

If she didn't look like she'd just caused a catastrophe, maybe her parents would go easier on her.

On her way back to the kitchen, Beatrice read her parents' faces.

It wasn't going to matter how much debris she'd removed from her hair, or how well she'd cleaned her face.

This wasn't going to be good news.

Beatrice plopped into her seat and braced herself.

Her mother spoke first. "For your own safety, we have to ground you."

Beatrice's chest clenched. She'd never been grounded before. "What does that mean?"

"No going up in trees," said her dad.

"No hanging by your knees," said her mother.

"And," her dad added, "we think you need a break from your ninja suit."

"For how long?"

Her mother frowned. "Indefinitely."

"We'll see how things go," said her dad.

Beatrice wasn't sure how long indefinitely was, but it sounded like a long time without her ninja suit.

Operation Upside was already under attack. Now her parents were trying to sabotage it too.

Her composure dissolved. All the tears she'd been holding in poured out. They fell like the rain had earlier. Loud and lots.

How was she supposed to prove Sam's innocence if she was grounded?

At the thought of Sam, Beatrice patted for her pocket.

Her crying stopped.

She was wearing clean, pocket-less pajamas. Her pocket—and Sam's note—was in the washing machine. With her ninja suit.

Without pausing for permission, Beatrice sprinted to the washer and threw open the lid. A blur of ninja-black whirred to a stop.

Beatrice dove into the drum and fished for her pants.

Just as her fingers found the pocket and closed around the paper, her dad's footsteps padded into the room.

"You're more than that ninja suit. I hope you know that," he said.

Beatrice clutched the outfit to her chest.

Partly in surprise, but mostly relief.

Sam's paper was damp, but still in one piece.

"I just needed to see it one more time."

"I understand." Her dad planted a kiss on her head, and gently returned her pants to the machine. "Why don't you go upstairs and spend some time with your sister? She was really worried about you."

15

JOLLY ROGER

The clank of pots and pans mingled with the murmur of her parents' voices in the kitchen. They had launched into a debate about the terms of her grounding as soon as she left the room.

Beatrice crawled up the stairway and peeked into the bedroom she shared with her sister.

Kate was curled on the lower bunk.

Headphones on.

Flash cards in hand.

Last week Kate had started a course that guaranteed she'd LEARN TO SPEAK LATIN IN JUST FIVE MINUTES A DAY. Kate now spent an hour each night mumbling with her headphones on.

Which was perfect, because Beatrice couldn't wait one more second to see what Sam had to say.

She dropped onto the top step—out of her sister's sight—and uncrumpled Sam's message.

Bewilderment replaced her curiosity.

She checked the front.

She checked the back.

She'd expected some secret communication.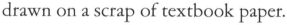

A mysterious code. But this was just a pirate flag, drawn on a scrap of textbook paper.

Then it hit her. This was Sam!

The Jolly Roger was not just a flag.

Flags were Sam's favorite secret language.

In the van, Sam had asked about her naval flag book, which was on Beatrice's top bunk, buried in a jumble of blankets.

Beatrice peeked around the corner and spied on Kate again.

She was still curled on her bed, lost in the world of Latin.

Beatrice tucked Sam's flag into her sock for safekeeping. If she was quiet enough, maybe she could get to her top bunk to grab Sam's book without catching Kate's attention.

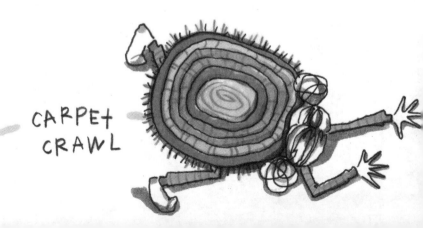

CARPET CRAWL

SLOW-MO
SPIN

She made it as
far as the ladder
before Kate removed
her headphones.

TiPTOE
TRANSFER

Beatrice paused.

Maybe Kate was only practicing her lesson.

"Quid agis?" Kate said the words louder this time. Her head peeked out at Beatrice. "In Latin, that means 'What in the world are you doing?'"

Beatrice glanced at the top bunk, where Sam's giant book of flags peeked from under her comforter. If she reached out her hand, she could touch it. Unfortunately, the Jolly Roger would have to wait.

Beatrice released the ladder and flipped to the floor.

"I didn't want to bother you," she told Kate.

Kate set her flash cards aside.

Her legs swung off the bed.

"How on earth did you miss the bus today?"

Yellow dots lined up in Beatrice's brain, then drove away. She shrugged. "I miscalculated."

Kate rolled her eyes.

"Speaking of calculating . . ." Beatrice flung her backpack around. "You're good at math, right?"

The question was rhetorical.

Kate was good at everything.

Beatrice unzipped her bag and yanked her math folder free. "Can you help me with this multiplication sheet? I don't want to bother Mom about anything tonight."

Kate flipped the folder open. *"Nolite ergo solliciti esse."* She grabbed one of her flash cards. "That's the main thing to remember about multiplication."

"Huh?"

"Don't let it freak you out."

Do not worry

Kate patted the mattress next to her. "Multiplication is like doing a bunch of addition really quickly. It helps you get bigger faster. And saves tons of time." She continued to rave about multiplication and all its benefits, but Beatrice didn't hear another word.

Her brain stopped at the word TIME.

Because her time was running out.

Kate bobbed in front of Beatrice's face. "Are you hearing any of this?"

Beatrice bit her lip. "Is there a kind of math that slows things down?"

"Why would anyone want that?"

That's the kind of math Beatrice needed right now. The kind that gave her more time to solve this mystery.

With Chloe's award missing and her ninja suit banned, how was she supposed to prove Sam's innocence by tomorrow?

Beatrice looked up at her sister. "Do you know what INDEFINITELY means?"

"It comes from the Latin." Kate brightened with enthusiasm. "*Indēfīnītus*. It means 'no fixed limit.'"

"Like—forever?"

It was worse than Beatrice guessed.

"Relax," said Kate. "You're the *felix culpa* queen."

"What's that mean?"

"That even when things go bad, somehow you turn them around."

A glow of hope flashed in Beatrice's cheeks.

If she could be a queen, that's the exact kind she'd choose to be.

Kate handed back her math. "Better ask Mom."

Beatrice grabbed the worksheet and climbed the ladder to her bed. Multiplication would have to wait. Right now, she had research to do.

16

AN EXTENSION

The next morning, Beatrice caught Lenny before school.

PSST...

"Lenny! Over here!" she hissed.

Yesterday, she needed an extraction from Sam.

Today, she needed an extension from Lenny.

After researching Sam's Jolly Roger flag last night, she was more certain than ever Sam had nothing to do with Chloe's award.

But to prove it, she needed more time.

Lenny dove into the bushes beside her. Accusation electrified her eyes. "You went back to the vet clinic yesterday, didn't you?"

"I had to."

"Everyone was freaking out," Lenny told her. "Kate called your mom crying when you weren't on the bus. Then your mom called my mom to see if you were with us. When the school didn't know where you were either, your dad wanted to call the police."

"Kate was crying?"

"You were missing. *Everyone* was crying." Lenny leaned closer. "What'd your parents say?"

Beatrice twirled a leaf. "They grounded me, and took my ninja suit away. . . ."

"I might have to talk to Mrs. Klein, too."

Lenny's eyes widened. "The principal?"

The first bell rang above their heads. Students scurried across the sidewalk and hurried inside.

"Did you get some clues at least?"

Beatrice shook her head. "Chloe's award was *gone*. Like it never existed."

Lenny winced. "Oh, yeah.... Chloe took it home last night."

"Chloe has it? How is that even possible?"

"I guess she stuck it in her clipboard after recess and put it in her bag before lunch. She wanted to show her mom." Lenny gestured behind them. "She just ran to the clinic to put it back."

Beatrice jumped up. "Really?"

Lenny pulled her down.

"Don't even think about it. You're in enough trouble already."

"Okay," Beatrice caved. "But I need another day."

"Why can't we just ask Sam if she did it?"

Mrs. Darzi's face popped into Beatrice's mind. She could still see the relief in her eyes that Sam had finally found a friend.

"Because she didn't do it." Beatrice dug into her backpack and fished out Sam's note. "Look what she gave me yesterday."

"A pirate flag?"

"It's the Jolly Roger." Beatrice hefted her backpack into her lap and grabbed Sam's book. "It's flag code, just like Bravo Zulu." She flipped through the pages. "See?"

Beatrice pointed at the entry. "In military code, a pirate flag means 'Mission Accomplished.'"

Lenny leaned over the page. Her finger jabbed the second definition. "Not in pirate code," she countered. "In pirate code, it means we're under attack!"

JOLLY ROGER
Traditional name for the well-known skull and crossbones pirate flag.

Beatrice sighed. "Sam's not a pirate. She's our friend—and her mission was a success. That's it." She tucked the flag into her jacket. "Can I have the extension, please? One more day?"

"Fine." Lenny exhaled dramatically. "Yes."

Beatrice dug out the cat ears from yesterday. "Can you still get me in?"

"Just be a regular cat, okay? Not some weird one from PBS."

17
PURE HAPPINESS

Beatrice couldn't concentrate on a word Mrs. Tamarack said all morning.

When recess arrived, the veterinary crowd flocked to the back of the playground like geese in formation.

Chloe walked out front, leading the way.

Her clipboard swung like a wing at her side.

Lenny lagged behind with Beatrice.

"Here's what we're going to do," she said. "While Chloe's signing everyone in, I'll sneak you through."

It wouldn't buy them tons of time.

But—if they worked fast—it might be enough.

Chloe stopped outside the entrance to the clinic. "Dogs on the right," she instructed. "Cats on the left."

Pretend canines and felines followed her lead and assembled in new formations.

Lenny smoothed her stethoscope and straightened her glasses. "Follow my lead."

Her stride cut left and wide.

Mustering an air of officiality, Lenny ignored Chloe and ushered Beatrice directly inside.

"Cat emergency," she called out. "Coming through." Her confident voice matched her all-business pace.

Chloe looked up from her clipboard.

Surprise punctuated her face.

With a nod of her chin, she noted Beatrice's fuzzy-eared headband and granted her approval.

Wes's gaze flicked up as the pair stalked past. He quirked an eyebrow, but didn't say a word.

REGULAR CAT.

Inside the clinic, Beatrice's heart leapt.

Chloe's award was back in its spot, just like Lenny claimed. Now proudly displayed in a glittering gold frame.

GLITTER!

UPSIDE

BEST VET

PRESENTED to:
CHLOE LLEWELYN

GOLD

Side by side, Beatrice and Lenny examined the evidence. Beatrice's nose hovered centimeters from Chloe's award, close enough to smell it.

"Come here," Beatrice whispered to Lenny.

"I *am* here," said Lenny.

"Closer," said Beatrice.

"What are we doing? Tasting it?"

"Just come here." She tugged Lenny forward. Their noses pressed against the paper. "Take a deep breath."

As Lenny inhaled, her eyes grew wide.

"I smell licorice!" she cried.

Beatrice clutched Lenny's hand.

"And maybe a hint of fruit punch?"

Together they grinned at Chloe's award.

Their eyes sparkled at the posters plastered next to it. Posters with remarkably similar lines, and the same assortment of smells.

Beatrice gripped Lenny's hand harder.

Lenny squeezed back.

Their feet danced with excitement. One name screamed silently between them, as close to telepathy as they could get.

Beatrice leaned her forehead against the wall, her body as boneless as a jellyfish.

The evidence proved what Beatrice already knew. Sam Darzi might be mysterious, but she was loyal, through and through.

"I'm glad it wasn't Sam."

Lenny's voice was quiet.

Apology tinged her words.

Then a question flashed across her face.

"Why would Wes sabotage Operation Upside, though?"

Sabotage didn't seem like Wes Carver.

Beatrice lifted her shoulder. "What if it wasn't sabotage?"

"What was it, then?"

"I don't know yet. . . ." Beatrice peeked out the window at Wes. "But I'll find out."

A throat cleared behind them.

"What are you two doing?" asked Chloe.

Beatrice and Lenny jumped apart.

The truth blurted from Beatrice's mouth. . . .

"We're looking at your award," she said.

A dreamy smile transformed Chloe's face. "I stared at it for hours last night." She leaned forward with a sigh. "It even smells good."

Beatrice grinned. "We just said the same thing."

The Best Vet of William Charles Elementary threw one arm around Beatrice, and the other around Lenny, and beamed.

Closing her eyes, Beatrice inhaled the words one more time. She didn't even like licorice, but today, it smelled like pure happiness.

18

ON A MISSION

Beatrice stepped from the shaded vet clinic into the morning light. The blinding glow of sunshine matched her happy mood.

"Wes?" she called out.

She expected to find him just outside the door.

His scented markers peppered the grass.

A half-done poster lay nearby.

Beatrice bent down and uncurled his current work-in-progress.

It seemed so obvious now.

Of course he had created Chloe's award.

Not only was Wes an artist, he also had an UPSIDE of his own to use as a pattern. Making awards would be a natural extension of his MOST THOUGHTFUL personality.

Humming a hip-hoppy tune, Beatrice followed a trail of markers around the corner, behind the clinic . . . and there he was.

Wes was bent low, crawling along the ground. His fingers foraged through the grass, searching for something.

It wasn't an unusual sight.

Before he was Chloe's assistant, Wes spent most recesses like this.

Alone in the grass. Combing for rocks.

Beatrice tried to hold in a smile.

"Hi," she chirped.

"Hey!" said Wes, when he noticed her. "No more cat?"

Beatrice stuffed her headband into her pocket and smiled. "Chloe sent me on a mission to find you."

Wes sat back on his heels. "I'm in the middle of a mission too."

"For rocks?"

Wes held up a magnifying glass. "For *clues.*"

He drew out the word dramatically.

That was one of the things Beatrice liked about Wes.

He understood certain words deserved to be said with dramatic effect.

"What are we looking for?" Beatrice squatted next to him.

"Can you keep a secret?"

Her heart sped up. "I love secrets."

Wes's voice dropped low. "You know how Chloe got that award yesterday?"

Beatrice nodded.

She tried to remain calm, but the smile on her face wouldn't cooperate.

Wes was going to tell her about the award.

In the distance, cheers rang across the soccer field. Wes jutted his chin toward the clinic. "I'm trying to solve the mystery."

Beatrice's excitement melted into confusion.

"Wait," she said. "What mystery?"

Wes scratched his nose. "I'm trying to figure out who made Chloe's award."

He wasn't making sense.

"Wasn't it *you*?"

His mouth fell open. "Me?"

It had to be him. The award smelled like licorice. And fruit punch.

And there was no way it was Sam.

Wes laughed. "It definitely wasn't me."

Blood rushed into her ears. "But it smells like your markers. . . ."

"I noticed that right away!" Wes exclaimed. "Which is why I made this." He reached into his sweatshirt pocket and flipped out a list.

Beatrice peeked over his shoulder. "These are your suspects?"

Wes smiled. "I call them leads."

He tapped the page. "It's everyone who had access to my markers last week."

Half their class was on the list.

One name stomped on Beatrice's hopes with a big black boot.

Her mouth went dry.

"Sam?" she croaked.

Wes lifted his shoulders. "It seems like something she would do."

He reached into his pocket and produced another piece of paper. "Last Friday, Sam borrowed my markers. Then she made me this."

Beatrice gulped.

The distinct scent of licorice drifted in the breeze. And it suddenly hurt to breathe.

Sam didn't do this.

She wouldn't.

Beatrice pushed the paper away. "Chloe could've made that award herself!"

Wes popped the cap off a marker. "That," he said, "is definitely worth considering."

He dashed Chloe's name onto the list.

Beatrice nudged his side. "Are you investigating this for Chloe? As her assistant?"

Wes stood up, blushing. "I'm investigating for personal reasons," he confessed. "A few weeks ago, I got one of these too."

The wind ruffled the pages of his notebook.

His eyes glinted in the sunshine.

"If I can figure out who gave Chloe *her* award, I'll know who made mine."

Wes was halfway there. He had a list of leads. If they solved the mystery together, maybe they could clear Sam's name.

There were risks, of course—but Beatrice didn't waste a second on any of them.

Her brain pushed aside all the ways the plan could go wrong, and focused on the one way it could go right.

"I'll help you figure it out," she told Wes.

"Really?"

"I'm very good at spying."

Wes laughed. "I believe you."

"But what if the person wants to stay anonymous?"

Mrs. Tamarack's whistle blared across the playground, and almost instantly, a pet stampede trampled out of the clinic.

Wes flipped his notebook closed. "I'll have to think about that. That sounds exactly like something Sam would say."

How was Beatrice going to tell Lenny the news?

If only she could put things back the way they used to be. Everything was so much better before Sam's loyalty was in question, back when Wes searched the grass for rocks, not incriminating clues.

19
TUESDAY AGAIN

Beatrice walked toward Classroom 3B in a daze.

The sun was high and bright, but a dark cloud followed her across the playground.

Behind her, Chloe and Lenny chattered with Eva, Grace, and Parvati.

Sam strolled several yards ahead with her sketchbook crooked under her arm.

A marker was tucked in the spiral spine.

Its licorice-black cap peeked from the top.

Was she being stubborn—
or stupid—to believe Sam
didn't make Chloe's award?

Outside the classroom
door, a tap on her
shoulder interrupted her
thoughts.

"Hey," said Chloe. She
fell into step beside her.
"What does your sister
have planned this week?"

Lenny appeared on Beatrice's other side,
grinning. "You forgot again, didn't you?"

Beatrice stopped in mid-stride.

Her eyes fixed on Lenny, hopeful and wide.

"Today's Tuesday?"

Every Tuesday, the Foreign Language Club gathered in the library during lunch. Her sister, Kate, was the founder and president, but Beatrice only joined the group because of Lenny.

Once again, Tuesday had snuck up on her, and the Foreign Language Club was the last thing on her mind. However, if Beatrice was lucky, Kate's club would be the *only* thing on Lenny's mind and she'd forget all about Wes.

The plastic seats near the podium were already filling up when they arrived. The library buzzed with the noise of transition. Crinkling bags, unzipping zippers, and snippets of conversations.

Sam was slouched in the already-crowded back row, crunching an apple while scribbling in a book. She seemed unaware of the commotion around her, but her eyes flicked up as Beatrice scooted down the row in front of her with Lenny and Chloe.

Sam's mouth tilted in a silent hello.

A smudge of ink stained the corner of her smile.

As Beatrice smiled back, her fingers found the pirate flag in her pocket. The phrase MISSION ACCOMPLISHED sailed through her mind.

Who'd gotten Sam's UPSIDE this week?

Besides Chloe, none of their classmates seemed especially giddy.

Kate tapped the microphone.

"Merci! Merci beaucoup!" she greeted everyone from the front. "Thank you for coming. I'm excited to announce what we're going to do."

Immediately, chattering ceased.

Everyone scrambled to their seats, and the screen behind Kate blinked to life.

"It's Let's Try Latin Day!" Kate held out a hat and swished her hand inside. "Each of you will receive a random Latin phrase to translate. We'll meet back here in ten minutes to discuss what your phrase means to you.

"We'll learn some Latin. And a little bit about each other." Kate shook the hat. The papers inside rustled with possibility. "Beatrice, do you want to start us off?"

Beatrice walked to the front and stuck her hand into the hat. Her fingers felt around, hoping to land on a good one.

Let's Try Latin Day
Latine Scriptor Experiri

She unfolded the paper and tried to make sense of the unfamiliar words.

Kate nudged her, "Read it out loud."

aut viam inveniam aut faciam

Beatrice stumbled over the letters as her sister clapped in approval.

"It's perfect for you."

It went like this as each person came forward.

Each person stumbled over their phrase.

Each time, Kate gushed with praise.

Once everyone had picked a paper, Kate pulled a rolling cart from behind the podium. "Mrs. Thomas pulled a bunch of books for us, plus we can use the computer lab." She glanced at the clock. "Be back at twelve thirty!"

Chloe leapt out of her seat and weaved up front to ask Kate a question.

Lenny tugged Beatrice's sleeve. "This way," she said. "Follow me."

Lenny led Beatrice across the library to a deserted corner of the computer lab. She looked like she wanted to talk, but Beatrice kept her head down and dropped into a seat.

Beatrice tossed her Latin phrase on the desk and roused her computer to life. "Kate didn't give us much time to look these up, did she?"

Her fingers fumbled over the keys and entered the mysterious words she'd drawn from the hat.

aut viam inveniam aut faciam

SEARCH

When the search results displayed, Beatrice grinned. Kate was right. The phrase was perfect.

Especially today.

Lenny scooted close. "I've been dying to ask you. . . ." Her eyes snapped with curiosity. "Why'd Wes do it? What'd he say?"

In the blue glow of the computer, Beatrice carefully copied each word of her definition and wiped her palms. When she finally faced her friend, she was calm.

"You should probably sit down."

20
WORST-CASE SCENARIO

Lenny clasped the arms of her chair. "I *am* sitting."

"Good," said Beatrice. "I have some news."

"What kind of news?"

The glare of the screen highlighted the worry in Lenny's eyes.

Beatrice took a deep breath.

"It wasn't Wes."

Lenny stood up, then she plopped back down. "I knew it was Sam. *I knew it.*"

"No way," said Beatrice. "Just because Wes didn't do it, doesn't mean Sam did."

Lenny stared hard.

Then she blinked a few times.

Probably *not* in Morse code, Beatrice decided.

"Let's stay calm," said Beatrice. "I know exactly what to do."

IT WORKS BEST UPSIDE DOWN....

Lenny eyed her warily.

"Trust me—this is going to work," Beatrice told her. "First, we need to close our eyes."

As Lenny's eyelids begrudgingly fluttered shut, Beatrice closed hers, too. "Now," she instructed. "Imagine all your worst fears are true."

"Okay . . ." Lenny nodded.

Beatrice peeked over. "You're doing it? You're imagining the absolute worst?"

"Yes," said Lenny through gritted teeth. "How is this going to help?"

Beatrice peered around the lab. The other students were lost in their own conversations.

No one was paying them any attention.

"Try saying your worst-case scenario out loud this time," she suggested.

Lenny's eyes flew open. "Out loud?"

"Just try."

"Fine. . . ." Her voice trembled. "The worst-case scenario is that Sam gave Chloe the BEST VET award. For revenge."

Lenny's glasses slipped down her nose.

"Remember when you gave Wes's award to Sam on accident? And how bad that made her feel? She knows our secret identities. She could ruin Operation Upside if she wanted to."

Lenny's words hung heavy in the air.

Beatrice let the awfulness of Lenny's scenario wash over her.

She let it wash over her like the time her family went to Florida, and a wave swelled up and pulled her under. It shoved her down and tossed her around, until her lungs felt like they were filled with salt water instead of air. She couldn't tell which way was up or out, and she wondered if she'd ever see the sky again.

Beatrice let herself feel it like that.

After several long seconds, which seemed like years, she popped above the water into blue sky. Alive, coughing, and wet.

Her lungs expanded in relief.

Beatrice nudged Lenny. "Feel any better yet?"

Anger blotched Lenny's face. "Out loud it sounded ten times *worse*. How could I possibly feel better?"

"Because," said Beatrice. "Even if the worst happened, we would survive."

Lenny stared at her, silent.

"I don't think we're going to lose Operation Upside," Beatrice continued. "But if we did, we'd invent something else to do."

Ideas instantly sprang to mind.

"Like, we could start a breakdancing crew!"

Lenny's stare turned into a glare.

"Or," Beatrice tried, "we could join Wes's detective agency."

For a moment, confusion replaced the frustration on Lenny's face. "Wes has a detective agency?" she asked.

Beatrice shrugged. "It's new."

Exasperated, Lenny jumped to her feet. "We need to talk to Sam *today*, Beatrice."

"You gave me an extension!"

Lenny shook her head. "The extension is off!" She snatched her things and bounded from the lab. Her dark curls swung after her as she stomped back to the meeting.

164

21

EVEN WORSE

Arguments stuck on Beatrice's tongue as Lenny marched away.

She wanted to beg Lenny to come back.

She wanted to share *her* worst-case scenario.

They would survive Lenny's. Even if they lost Operation Upside—and Sam's friendship—she and Lenny would still have each other.

But there was a scenario worse than Sam's betrayal.

Beatrice's worst-case scenario was that Sam was innocent—that she didn't give Chloe the award, that she never sabotaged Operation Upside—but Lenny accused her anyway.

Sam was just starting to trust them.

If Lenny confronted her now, nothing would ever be the same.

Operation Upside might survive, but their friendship with Sam wouldn't. Even if their friendship with Sam did survive somehow, Sam shouldn't *have* to survive that.

Beatrice scooped up her things and rushed after Lenny. She ran so fast, her feet barely touched the ground.

She needed to reach Sam first.

Beatrice jumped a row of chairs, overtook Lenny, and dove into the empty seat next to Sam just as Kate announced, *"Tempus est scriptor! Time's up!"*

Hi!

Sam's chair rocked in the aftermath.

Lenny perched on a chair next to Chloe, chewing her thumb, and watched Beatrice from the corner of her eye.

Kate smiled at the crowd. "Chloe has kindly volunteered to go first."

Applause spattered through the crowd as Chloe approached the podium.

She adjusted the mic to match her height and then said, *"Dura a nobis non timentur."* Her Latin words sang out confidently. "'Don't be afraid of a difficult thing.'"

The definition crinkled in her hands. "This one reminds me of my life." Her voice wobbled, like she was trying not to cry.

Her usual confidence slipped away.

"I moved over the summer. I didn't think I could do it, but—" Her throat bobbed, and her eyes landed on Lenny. "Even though I'm homesick . . . everyone's been really nice. I even got an award this week."

Kate applauded. "Thank you, Chloe. I love that quote too." She searched the room. "Who's next?"

Chloe sat down and nudged Lenny in the ribs.

Lenny bit her lip and trudged to the podium. Her fingers smoothed the paper. "*De omnibus dubitandum*. . . . 'Be suspicious of everything.'" She narrowed her eyes. "I like this advice. It seems very wise."

Beatrice glanced at Sam. She had Wes's marker uncapped, her attention on the page in front of her.

Lenny's stare shifted to Beatrice.

"Being an optimist can be dangerous. If you're wrong, the cost could be high." Her eyes dared Beatrice to argue. "It's better to be safe than sorry."

"Merci," Kate thanked her. "Food for thought, for sure."

After that, volunteers took turns coming forward, until Kate finally said, "We're almost out of time. Let's do just one more."

She looked around.

"Beatrice?"

Next to Beatrice, Sam shut her book. "I'll go," Sam said suddenly.

The whole room jolted with surprise as Sam's boots shuffled to the front.

"I got *'Amicitia pulchra est.'*" A lock of hair swooped over one eye. "It means 'Friendship is beautiful.'" She opened her book and produced a sheet of paper. "I made a poem about it."

She tucked her hair back, swallowed, and began. Words rolled off her tongue, both soft and strong, like one of Beatrice's break-beat songs.

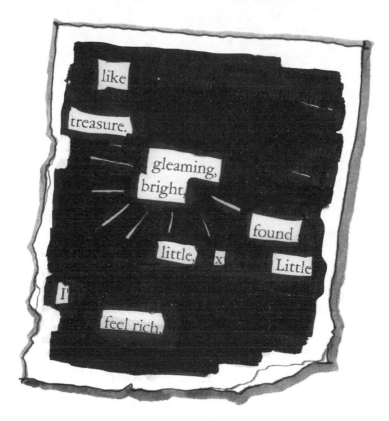

like

treasure.

gleaming,
bright.

found

little,   x   Little

I

feel rich.

Wonder hovered in the silence.

Beatrice's skin prickled with life.

She looked at Lenny, trying to telegraph, *See?*

Sam gave them each a nod as she angled back to her seat.

Kate clapped enthusiastically. *"Perfectus! Perfectus!"* She leaned into the microphone. "Perfect end to our day."

As the meeting closed, a small crowd circled around Sam, asking about her poem. Beatrice stood guard to intercept Lenny if she tried to approach.

"I just go with my gut," Sam told them. "I hide all the words that don't belong, and almost like magic, a poem shows up."

When the swarm eventually slipped away, Sam leaned toward Beatrice. "Is Lenny okay?"

Beatrice was afraid to look.

"Why?"

"She's been looking at me weird all day."

Beatrice shrugged. "Don't worry. That's how she always looks at me."

LiKE THAT ⟶

The rest of the afternoon, Beatrice worked hard to keep Lenny far from Sam.

She couldn't keep them apart forever, though.

She needed a plan.

Beatrice unfolded her unused scrap of Latin.

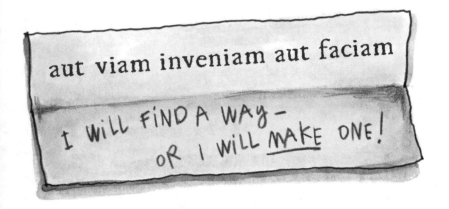

aut viam inveniam aut faciam

I WILL FIND A WAY — OR I WILL MAKE ONE!

22

AUT VIAM INVENIAM AUT FACIAM

When second recess arrived, Beatrice marched outside. Since the trees were off-limits while she was grounded, she planted herself in the grass next to Chloe's clinic, where she could keep an eye on both Lenny and Sam, and flipped into thinking position.

← LENNY   SAM →

Good ideas came to Beatrice all the time.

They struck like magic, especially when she was upside down.

Today was no different.

Except today, instead of waiting for an idea to strike, she planned to force one out.

Wes collapsed beside her, devoid of his usual energy. "Hey," he said.

Beatrice lowered her voice. "Any luck with your leads?"

"None." He flopped onto his back. His arm draped over his face. "It's still a really long list."

"There *has* to be a different way to look at it."

"No," Wes mused. "Maybe you were right. Maybe these awards are meant to be anonymous." He perked up. "Maybe I'm supposed to pass it on, and do something nice for someone else instead."

It was a nice idea—a very Wes idea—but for Beatrice, giving up wasn't an option.

This was a *make*-a-way kind of day.

As Wes organized his art supplies, Beatrice begged her brain to work.

AIR FLARE

She thought high.

THE WORM

She thought low.

She thought fast.

HEAD
SPIN

And she thought slow.

THINKER
FREEZE

Before long, her vigorous thinking jarred Sam's Jolly Roger from her pocket. Beatrice gasped as she caught it in her fist.

"Wes?" she asked excitedly. "Do you have your list?!"

Hesitantly, he retrieved his notebook.

"May I borrow a marker?"

With a flick of his wrist, options fanned out like a magic trick. "Sure," he said. "Take your pick."

Beatrice didn't hesitate. "Definitely that one."

Beatrice uncapped the marker with her teeth, and analyzed their leads.

"I have an idea," she said. "What if we cross off everyone who *isn't* it to find out who *is*? Like one of Sam's blackout poems."

Wes's eyebrows drew together. "Isn't that what we've been doing?"

Beatrice pressed the marker to the page. "Not exactly."

Dark ink crissed and crossed and filled in the empty spaces, until only names were left.

Wes chewed the end of his marker nervously. He winced whenever Beatrice made another mark. "This doesn't seem very scientific," he observed. "That's my only copy."

"I'm going with my gut," she told him.

Beatrice couldn't hang from her favorite tree, but she could still go out on a limb.

Concentration crinkled her brow as she studied the names. In six quick swipes, the soccer crowd disappeared.

Martin, Quinn, and Ola B.

Then Jetta, Angelo, and Emma Dorsey.

The back of the playground didn't even exist for them. Making a BEST VET award seemed highly unlikely.

Her marker hovered over the page. "What about Eva? What colors did she borrow?"

Wes scrunched his face. "Watermelon and Cherry, I think."

SOMETHING PINK....

In one stroke, Eva disappeared.

"Parvati and Justine?"

Wes hesitated. "Um . . . black and green."

He leaned over, nabbed the marker, and covered their names in black. He returned the marker to Beatrice and shrugged. "They gave them right back."

Beatrice blacked out Chloe's name next. She was never *really* a suspect.

After that, only two names remained.

Wes pointed at the list. "It wasn't Grace," he said. "She was at the orthodontist."

Beatrice remembered Sam's words back in the library: how she hides all the words that don't belong, to magically uncover the words that do.

Trusting her gut, Beatrice pressed the marker down one last time.

Wes gasped. "Why did you do that?"

"Because," said Beatrice, "Sam's name doesn't belong on the list."

Wes's mouth dropped. "But Grace wasn't even around!"

"Exactly," said Beatrice. "A perfect alibi. What if she put up Chloe's award *before* her appointment and slipped back after lunch?"

A triumphant gleam sparkled in her eyes.

"Was she even in school Monday morning?" asked Wes.

Beatrice bit her lip.

"I need to double-check."

A hunch and a blackout poem wouldn't be enough to convince Lenny.

She needed concrete proof.

To prove her theory, she needed a peek at the sign-out sheet in the school office. She only had a couple minutes to come up with a convincing ploy to see Ms. Cindy, the school nurse.

She smiled at Wes. "Do I look sick to you?"

23
OPPORTUNITY

When Beatrice stepped into the classroom, Mrs. Tamarack crossed her arms over her chest, like she could read her mind.

"Beatrice," she instructed. "Come here, please." She crooked her finger and motioned Beatrice forward.

Beatrice gulped.

She hadn't even done anything yet.

Mrs. Tamarack pulled out a pink slip of paper and adjusted her glasses. "Mrs. Klein would like to see you in her office." She peeked over her spectacles. "Bring your backpack, just in case."

Beatrice's fingers shook as she took the paper.

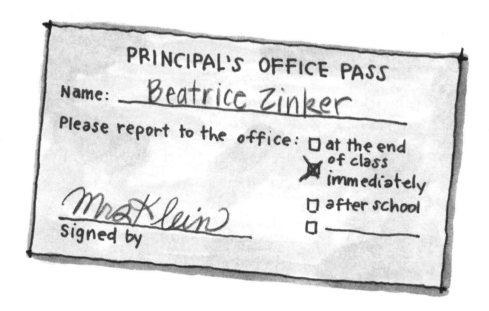

Even though her parents had warned her, and she knew it was a possibility, nothing can prepare you for the sight of your name on a note from the principal.

Sam shot her a sympathetic smile.

Instantly, Beatrice's mission flooded back.

She glanced at Mrs. Klein's summons and grinned. Occasionally, when you need a plan, life hands you a personalized invitation.

Sneaking into the main office of William Charles Elementary was practically impossible.

Floor-to-ceiling glass formed the facade, like an aquarium. Approaching visitors were visible all the way down the hall.

Especially grounded visitors whose ninja suits were indefinitely packed away.

In her ninja suit, Beatrice felt invincible and invisible. In her bright track suit, she still felt unstoppable—but also completely unmissable.

"Beatrice Zinker!" Ms. Cindy cheered when she saw her. "My favorite upside down thinker!" The school nurse turned to the woman sitting at a desk behind her. "I'll take care of this one, Harriet."

Mrs. Woods, the school secretary, harrumphed at her computer screen. "She had this place in a tizzy yesterday."

Beatrice cringed. "Sorry."

Ms. Cindy leaned against the counter. "I'm just glad you're okay." The sign-out sheet rested only inches from the nurse's elbow. "So, my dear," she asked. "What brings you in today?"

Beatrice held out her invitation.

Ms. Cindy's eyebrows rose. "You've been summoned." She winked. "I'll let Mrs. Klein know you're here."

As Ms. Cindy marched toward Mrs. Klein's door, Beatrice took a deep breath.

Nerves twisted in her gut.

Even Mrs. Klein's door was frightening.

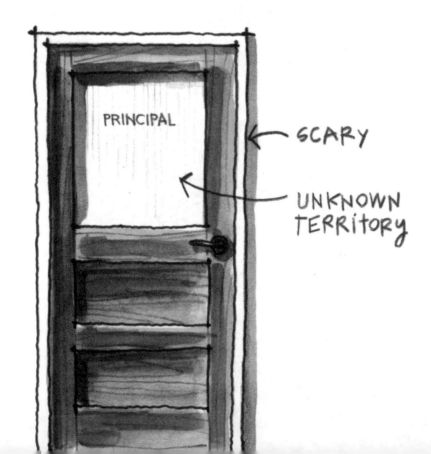

It was solid wood with a frosted window. You couldn't see any details through the milky glass, just enough movement to make you wonder what horrors were happening inside.

Beatrice forced herself to think of Sam.

Even when nerves hit, spies stick to their plans.

She pushed up her sleeves and took a giant step to the right, directly in front of the sign-out sheet. Heart pounding, Beatrice picked up the clipboard.

A surprising number of people came in and out of the building each day.

Today's log was almost full.

Monday's was long gone.

It was flipped over the top of the clipboard, a few pages back.

Beatrice leafed through the previous pages, searching for Monday, hunting for Grace.

When she found the entry, her breath caught.

Her blackout poem proved true.

Monday morning, Grace signed out at 10:14 a.m. It would've been easy to hang Chloe's award as she left for her orthodontist appointment, and then to return during lunch, completely undetected.

Beatrice stared at Grace's signature scrawled across the line. The *i* in BENJAMIN made her want to flip cartwheels in the middle of the office.

DAY	STUDENT NAME	OUT	
Mon	André Kovac		
Mon	Nevaeh Frost		
Mon	Esmé Fields	9:42	
mon.	Grace Benjamin	9:55	12:0
Mon	Terrence Allen	10:03	
MON.	IBRAHIM SAEED	10:14	12:15
Mon.	Serena Ramírez	11:30	1:40
Mon.		12:00	

The dot on top looked like a tiny little heart. Beatrice had seen one just like it before.

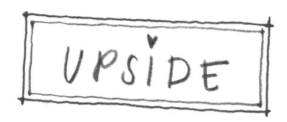

On Chloe's UPSIDE award.

Sabotage usually requires three things: means, motive, and opportunity.

The sign-out sheet proved Grace had opportunity to deliver Chloe's award. Her use of Wes's marker and her heart-dotted handwriting proved she had the means.

But what about Grace's motive?

Why would she want to sabotage Operation Upside?

Beatrice tapped the pen on the clipboard, thinking. Mrs. Woods piped up from her desk. "There's no need to sign in, dear. You're quite unmissable."

The clipboard clattered from Beatrice's fingers just as the principal's door swung open.

Ms. Cindy strode out with Mrs. Klein, the principal, and Mr. Hannah, the school counselor, trailing behind her.

Mrs. Klein offered her hand. "It's good to see you, Beatrice." She pointed a thumb behind her. "We're still cleaning up a luncheon in my office. Mr. Hannah suggested you might be more comfortable talking in his office anyway, where you're more familiar. How would you feel about that?"

Beatrice nearly collapsed in relief.

"Good," she answered while trying to keep the smile off her face. "I'd feel good."

Ms. Cindy flipped the light switch in her shared office with Mr. Hannah and ushered Beatrice inside. "Good luck," she mouthed.

Once they were seated, Mrs. Klein took the lead. "You're not in trouble, Beatrice, but we need to talk about what happened yesterday."

Beatrice nodded.

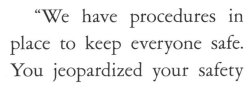

"We have procedures in place to keep everyone safe. You jeopardized your safety by wandering away."

Mr. Hannah leaned forward. "Is there a reason you walked off in the rain?"

"Yes." Mrs. Klein nodded. "Mrs. Tamarack said your class plays some veterinarian game?"

"Recess was canceled, and I really needed to get outside." Beatrice glanced at the clock on Mr. Hannah's desk. "I thought there was enough time."

Mr. Hannah's head bobbed. "It's hard to sit all day," he agreed.

"But safety comes first, do you understand?" Mrs. Klein shifted in her seat.

Beatrice thought of the looks on her parents' faces when they spun into the driveway. She remembered how awful it felt to see the buses drive away.

"I understand," she said.

Mrs. Klein's speech continued, sprinkled with words like RULES, RESPONSIBILITY, and ROUTINES. But as the principal spoke, something on the bulletin board behind her grabbed Beatrice's full attention. As it crystallized into focus, Mrs. Klein's voice dissolved into the background.

Mr. Hannah's bulletin board was a collage of motivational posters, student drawings, and sticky notes. Tacked in the middle, right next to Mr. Hannah's college diploma and his counseling certificate, was a very familiar document.

Happiness jolted through Beatrice.

Sam didn't give her award to Chloe!

She gave her award to Mr. Hannah!

Beatrice needed to find Lenny immediately. She needed to tell her about the award Mr. Hannah got and—more importantly—she needed to tell her about Grace Benjamin's happy, heart-shaped dot!

Mrs. Klein cleared her throat. "Do you have any concerns about that arrangement, Beatrice?"

Beatrice pulled her gaze from Mr. Hannah's UPSIDE. Her eyes bounced from her principal to her counselor and back again.

What arrangement?

Mr. Hannah offered a broad, encouraging grin. "We think the buddy system will be good for both of you."

Mrs. Klein held out her hand. "Do we have a deal?"

Shaking on a deal you know nothing about isn't wise, but when you're on a mission, compromises are necessary sometimes.

This was one of those times.

Their meeting was running long, the day was running short, and more than two hours ago, Lenny had run out of patience.

Beatrice shook her principal's hand.

"Deal," she said.

"Wonderful." Mrs. Klein scribbled a pass. "Let's get you to class." She smiled. "No detours, please."

Beatrice hitched her backpack into place and smiled. "No detours," she agreed. "I'll go straight back."

She might even run.

Mr. Hannah handed her another note. "Please give this one directly to Mrs. Tamarack."

Beatrice clutched both papers in her fist.

As Ms. Cindy waved good-bye, Beatrice raced out of the office and straight toward Lenny, trying to beat the clock.

OFFICE

While class was in
session—and Mrs. Tamarack
was teaching—Lenny and Sam were
safely apart. Once the bell rang, Sam
was fair game.

24
BETTER THAN WE DREAMED

The door to Classroom 3B swung open as Beatrice bounded down the hall.

"Walking feet!" Mrs. Tamarack called.

With a sigh, Beatrice slowed her stride.

"I'm glad you made it back before the bell." Mrs. Tamarack kicked the doorstop into place. "I have homework for you."

Focused on finding Lenny, Beatrice followed her teacher inside. Though the bell hadn't rung, everyone was out of their seats.

The veterinary crew swarmed around Grace's desk, bobbing with excitement. Their high-pitched squeals drew a scolding glare from Mrs. Tamarack. Lenny stood among them, frozen and pale-faced.

Mrs. Tamarack pointed at Beatrice's right hand, where she still clutched the pass from Mrs. Klein and the pink paper from Mr. Hannah. "Are those for me?"

Beatrice glanced down, distracted, as Mrs. Tamarack exchanged her papers for a homework packet. While Mrs. Tamarack skimmed the note, Beatrice swept the room for Sam.

Sam, who gave her UPSIDE to Mr. Hannah.

Sam, who was never trying to sabotage Operation Upside.

What if she was too late?

What if Lenny had already accused Sam of sabotaging them?

Mrs. Tamarack waved Mr. Hannah's pink paper in the air and yelled, "Sam! Grab your backpack. Time to go!"

Sam emerged from the coat closet, yellow bag in tow. When their eyes met, relief soared through Beatrice.

Sam raised her eyebrows. "How'd it go?"

"Better than expected."

Mrs. Tamarack clucked her tongue. "Your turn, Sam." She presented the request from Mr. Hannah. "Looks like we'll see you tomorrow."

It was Beatrice's turn to offer a supportive smile.

As Sam slipped away and Mrs. Tamarack strode off to settle an argument across the room, Lenny snagged Beatrice's elbow and pulled her aside. "Operation Upside is ruined! Two more people got UPSIDES!"

Beatrice's eyes flew across the room. "Who?"

"Grace got *another* one. And Eva got one too." Lenny stepped into the coat closet and snatched her backpack from the rack. "Why would Sam do this?!"

From his desk, Wes flashed a thumbs-up in Beatrice's direction. His gesture confirmed what Beatrice had already guessed.

Wes was responsible for one—maybe *both*—of the newest UPSIDE awards. He was trying to act composed, but his face glowed with the joy of doing something kind.

Next to Beatrice, Lenny was still freaking out. "I *knew* I should've talked to her," she muttered. "How could she?!"

Beatrice gripped Lenny's shoulders as realization hit her. "Lenny!" she breathed. "I finally understand multiplication!"

Lenny's head tilted sideways. "What?!"

Beatrice looked at Wes's beaming thumbs-up and at the happy faces gathered around their awards, and finally, the math made sense.

"Operation Upside isn't ruined," she exclaimed. "It's the opposite! It's working better than we dreamed!"

Above them, the bell blared.

Mrs. Tamarack peered around the corner. "Let's continue this conversation in the corridor, girls." She steered them out the door and into the hallway with the rest of the class.

Beatrice zigzagged through the crowded hall and ducked into a drinking fountain alcove.

Lenny stuck close and mirrored her every move. "I don't understand what's going on," she complained.

"Sam didn't sabotage us," said Beatrice. "She gave her UPSIDE to Mr. Hannah."

"She didn't?" Lenny narrowed her eyes. "Who gave Chloe that award, then?"

Beatrice dropped her voice.

"Grace did."

Shock drained Lenny's face.

"*GRACE* sabotaged us?!"

Beatrice shook her head. "It wasn't sabotage," she said. "Your award made her happy. She was just passing it on."

Up ahead, Grace and Eva grinned. Lenny pointed at the awards in their hands. "What about those? Who are those from?"

"I think Wes gave one to Grace," said Beatrice.

Lenny was silent as she stared down the hall. Her forehead wrinkled, like the wheels of her brain were working overtime.

"Here comes Chloe!" Beatrice whispered. "Take a drink!"

They ducked their mouths over the waterspouts until Chloe was a safe distance ahead. When the coast was clear, Lenny wiped the water from her mouth. "What about the other one?"

Beatrice shrugged. "I don't know. Wes too? Chloe, maybe?"

Wes grinned at Beatrice as she and Lenny stepped through the double doors that led outside. Beatrice had so many questions for him, but they would have to wait.

"See you at recess tomorrow?"

"Of course," said Wes.

Beatrice smiled back. "Good."

As they stepped onto the sidewalk, Lenny was oddly quiet.

"I thought you'd be happy," said Beatrice.

Lenny bit her thumb. "You always say I see the best in everyone, but this time . . ." Her voice got tiny. "I think I was jealous."

Her quiet confession was barely audible.

"Sam lives across the street from you." Lenny's footsteps slowed to a stop. "She sees you all the time, and I don't get to. . . ."

Beatrice nodded. "That's exactly how I feel about Chloe."

They stood in silence, side by side, as the after-school crowd funneled around them.

Beatrice interrupted the moment with a jab in Lenny's side. "Hey—do you know where we can find a typewriter around here?"

"Here? Today?" Lenny gaped. "Aren't you in enough trouble?"

Beatrice laughed. "It's for something good."

Conspiracy twinkled in Lenny's eyes. "I know where we can get a typewriter. But not today, and not here." Grinning, she whispered her idea into Beatrice's ear.

"You're a genius," Beatrice declared.

"We'd have to wait for the weekend. . . ."

Beatrice nodded. "It'll be worth the wait."

A third shadow joined theirs on the sidewalk.

"Are you guys meeting without me?" Sam's face popped between their shoulders. "I was hoping I'd find you, Beatrice. Mr. Hannah says we're bus buddies now."

Bus buddies?

Sam's eyes were hopeful. "He said you agreed to it?"

"Oh," said Beatrice.

The mysterious agreement she'd made with Mrs. Klein came rushing back.

Still, she was confused.

She pointed at Sam. "You never take the bus, though."

Sam pulled a pass from her pocket. "I do now," she announced. "It's a long story."

In front of them, a line of buses rumbled in place. Sam nodded at one. "I believe this is us?" she said.

Lenny gestured at the next in line, where Chloe was waving. "And that one's me!"

She reached over to hug Beatrice, and then skipped to her waiting bus.

25

LITTLE BY LITTLE

Lenny wiped her palms on her jeans. "I can't believe we're really doing this."

"Me either," said Beatrice.

They put their fingertips together and pressed the button.

Ding. Dong.

The muffled sound of the doorbell trilled inside the house.

Beatrice gripped her duffel bag.

Lenny adjusted her glasses.

They rocked on their toes, waiting.

Soon the lock jiggled.

Then the doorknob turned.

A smiling Mrs. Darzi opened the door. "Beatrice!" she greeted. "What a wonderful surprise." She held out her hand to Lenny. "I'm Sam's mom."

Lenny reached out. "I'm Lenny."

Mrs. Darzi motioned them inside. "Come on in."

The girls stepped over the threshold into the Darzis' tiny foyer.

Sam's black boots sat on a mat near the door.

Mrs. Darzi looked up at the ceiling and called, "Sam! Your friends are here!"

Floorboards squeaked overhead. Shuffling footsteps creaked down the stairs, until Sam appeared on the bottom step.

It was a Sam they'd never seen before.

Her dark hair was in a ponytail, pulled away from her face. Instead of her brother's boots, she was wearing fuzzy slippers shaped like lobsters.

"Hi, guys." Her fingers lifted in a tiny wave. "Is everything okay?"

"Everything's fine," Beatrice assured her. "I was just wondering—can I borrow your typewriter? You know that project I was working on? I finally made up my mind...."

Sam's eyes widened. "Oh," she said. "Sure." She shrugged at her mom. "Can they come up?"

"Of course," Mrs. Darzi beamed.

Beatrice and Lenny discarded their shoes next to Sam's boots and joined her on the stairs.

Lenny pointed at Sam's fuzzy feet. "I didn't know you liked lobsters."

Sam laughed. "Wait until you see my room."

"She's not kidding," Mrs. Darzi called after them. "It's a sight to behold."

In Sam's doorway, they paused and beheld the sight. A large-scale lobster print wrapped Sam's entire room. Lobster artwork dotted the walls. And her bookshelves overflowed with lobster trinkets of all shapes and sizes.

Sam shrugged. "I think they're cute." She pointed at the giant lobster that took up half her bed. "That's Lizzie."

"They *are* cute," said Beatrice.

Sam went to the table under her window and lugged the typewriter into her lap. Her eyes smiled at Beatrice. "You finally decided, huh?"

Beatrice nodded. "It took a while."

She unzipped her duffel bag and handed Sam her blank certificate. Lenny folded herself onto the mattress, right next to Lizzie the lobster.

Sam twisted the typewriter knob, and the paper inched into the machine. "So," she said. "What am I typing?"

Certainty straightened Beatrice's spine. "It should say, MOST WORTH GETTING TO KNOW."

Sam's eyebrow quirked up, but her fingers punched the keys without question.

TAP
TAP

Stroke by stroke, capital letters stamped across the page. Once Sam typed the last *W,* she looked up. "Who's it for? I'm so curious."

Beatrice peered over Sam's shoulder as she aligned the guide. Lenny scooted to the edge of the bed.

"I'll spell it," Beatrice said.

Sam's fingers danced in expectation.

"Okay," said Beatrice. "The first letter is *S.*"

Sam typed an *S.*

"Next an *A.*"

An *A* inked onto the page.

"Then *M,*" Beatrice told her.

Sam's fingers waited for the next letter. Lenny hid a gigantic grin behind one of Lizzie's claws. When Beatrice didn't continue, Sam's eyes snapped up, confused.

"Wait," said Beatrice. "What's your middle name?"

Sam shook her head. "I don't have one."

Beatrice nodded and continued spelling.

She spoke each letter slowly, a dramatic pause between each one. "The last name is D... A... R... Z..."

At Z, Beatrice stopped talking because Sam wasn't typing anymore. She was staring at the page. As still as a statue.

The partially typed name sat between them—unfinished, but saying so much.

When Sam finally spoke, her voice was cautious. "This is for me?"

Beatrice reached over Sam at the typewriter and plinked the final letter of her name. Then, with a flourish, she presented the award to Sam.

"For you," she said.

Lenny hugged the lobster to her chest. "From both of us."

Beatrice reached into her pocket. "We also made you these."

This poem is a flag that means friendship that means rooftops and even doorbells

Through green glasses or not You are true blue

Sam swallowed. "I don't know what to say." Her eyes shone with emotion.

"It's okay," said Beatrice. "I'm learning telepathy."

At the end of a long week, here they were. The three of them—together.

Chloe's award wasn't an act of sabotage. It wasn't even a catastrophe. It was a triumph.

Operation Upside was working.

Really working.

Their tiny operation was making a difference. Just like multiplication, it was spreading faster than Beatrice could comprehend.

Beatrice grabbed their hands. Sam on her right. Lenny on her left. "We're doing it, guys."

Little by little, they were doing something big.

Acknowledgments

Every book is a collaboration of countless hands, hearts, and minds. Much gratitude to my incredible editor, Rotem Moscovich, who encouraged me to follow my instincts with this one, and to the entire Disney Hyperion team who help make Beatrice her best—especially Heather Crowley, Phil Buchanan, Sara Liebling, Jerry Gonzalez, Melissa Lee, Amy Goppert, Dina Sherman, and each copy editor.

Infinite thanks to my agent, Stephen Barr, for being Beatrice's true north and for relentlessly seeing the upside in every situation. I'm also grateful to Cecilia de la Campa, Andrea Vedder, Nora Long, and the whole team at Writers House for all they do on my behalf.

To my friends and family: Thank you for your cheers, check-ins, and love. Giant hugs to the educators, librarians, booksellers, readers, and fellow writers who've championed Beatrice. I couldn't do it without you.

High fives to Bob, Matthew, and Nolan, my favorite trio and stellar in-house consultants. Love you, buddies.